THE HUMAN

THE HUMAN

AN ADAM KINDE ALTERNATE FUTURE
MYSTERY

K. R. WATTS

STUART TARTLY PRESS

Stuart Tartly Press
17216 Saticoy Street, #226
Lake Balboa, CA 91406-2103

ISBN: 978-1-953595-07-2

For those who have struggled to discern good from evil.

Any sufficiently advanced technology is indistinguishable from magic.

— Arthur C. Clarke

Chapter 1

"Why Adam Kinde? He was the son of a servant, a member of the clergy, to all appearances the most ordinary of men."

Silas Redford, *The Real Adam Kinde: An Experiment in Biography*

SOMETHING about her didn't make sense.

I was a young man at the time, not a year out of seminary, single and struggling with my new role as pastor. I was enjoying my normal Thursday routine, writing the first draft of the next week's sermon over lunch at The Humble Monk. That's the *original* Humble Monk, which claimed to have been in operation over three hundred years—since the last days of the Dark Age. Around the time of President John McCain in the early 21st century, before the second coming of Joshua.

The aroma of freshly baked cinnamon buns floated from

the bakery case, while the music blaring from the restaurant's Bible completely failed to drown out the clatter of plates, pans, and silverware from the kitchen.

It was the National Gospel Quartet, belting out a medley of traditional classics. They had just finished "Are Ye Able" and segued into "All You Need Is God" when I glanced up, my stylus suspended in mid-sentence over the screen of my Bible, and saw her.

She paused, just inside the door, and surveyed the room.

The Gospel quartet sang:

"All you need is God..."

It took me a moment to figure out what bothered me about her.

She wore her brown hair short, with a thin strip shaved down the center: stylish, but not extreme, and clearly professionally done. Her blouse was conservative as well. One shoulder bare, the other padded—not the height of fashion, but not completely out of date.

"All you need is God, God..."

Her eyes were hazel: intelligent and calm as she glanced from one table to another.

But her forehead was blank.

"God is all you need."

There were only two kinds of adults who didn't wear a logo. Holders, because they didn't have to, and infidels, because they had no right to.

Mine—the triple *F*s of the Fellowship of Free Fundamentalists—was proudly tattooed above my left eyebrow. Non-clerics like the proprietor of The Humble Monk wore the Logo of their patron—in his case, the Franklyn Corporation—above the right.

Her eyebrows, slightly bushy and the same soft brown as her hair, had only the clear skin of her forehead above them.

She was about my age, perhaps a little younger, maybe twenty or twenty-two.

"There's nothing God can't do that can be done…"

She was too well dressed and well groomed to be an infidel. But I was sure I would have recognized any holder who made their way that far inside Franklyn territory.

I forgot about my sermon. I can't stand an unsolved puzzle.

I put my stylus down, lost in thought, then realized that she was returning my gaze.

She smiled.

There are all sorts of smiles you can get from a woman. There's the smile of condescension you receive from a holder's wife or daughter. There's the seductive smile you get from the bored parishioner who may or may not mean it. There's the cautious and slightly pitying smile you get from your friends' wives when you visit for dinner without a spouse or date. There's the deferential smile on the faces of the committee woman from your congregation.

This smile was like none of those. It had no hint of rank, no hint of invitation or fear. And yet there was nothing at all masculine about it.

It was the completely open and frank smile of a social equal.

I froze, caught off guard—something that rarely happened to me. I was tempted to look away, to pretend that I hadn't been looking at her at all. But there was something so generous in her smile, so friendly in her eyes, that it seemed rude to ignore her.

"It's eaaasy . . ."

I managed a non-committal nod of acknowledgment, and her smile subtly shifted. I couldn't put my finger on exactly *how* it shifted, but it did. It was no longer just a friendly smile. It was amused.

Underneath the smile, she was laughing.

I expected to be embarrassed by that, or offended, but found that I wasn't. And then I realized why I wasn't.

She wasn't laughing at me, she was laughing with me, inviting me to share the humor of our awkward moment.

I found myself returning the same amused smile.

Then she returned my nod, and turned her attention to the proprietor, who was offering to seat her.

Relieved, I picked up my stylus and refocused on my sermon. Or tried to.

I still couldn't let it go.

Everything about her—her haircut, her clothes, the fact that the proprietor (a well known snob) would seat her personally—*everything* indicated that she was a holder. Most of all, the complete lack of a logo.

But I had never heard of her, and she had treated me as an equal. Boyd Franklyn did that, or at least came close most of the time, but that was different. We grew up together. You wouldn't catch him treating a stranger like that.

The Quartet had segued into their next tune.

"The earth is not my home,
I'm just passing through . . ."

I sneaked another peek as the proprietor seated her across

the room, and she seemed to be treating him with the same respect.

Curious.

Then she tugged at one of her fingernails, and the mystery was solved.

Chapter 2

"It's a common mistake to assume that angels, and guardian angels in particular, were common during the short domination. With few exceptions they were a privilege of the privileged—distinguished members of the clergy or particularly powerful political figures. The average squatter might go a lifetime without sighting one in person."

Dorothy Kenning, *The Short Domination: A Student Primer.*

IN MY DEFENSE, I wasn't at my best that day. I'd made two promises that morning, and wished I hadn't made either.

I had risen early, and set out on foot to the Lindley Retreat House to visit my father. I preferred not to use my personal chariot when venturing into squatter territory unless I was on official church business. Not that my superiors would have objected. There was nothing especially pretentious about it: a one-man platform without a seat. But I felt personal use of ordinary miracles—aside from my Bible and altar, of course— put a distance between me and those in my flock, who didn't have access to such advantages.

It was a clear morning, and the roads were dry, which was normal for the San Fernando Valley. There was a chill in the air. Some of the leaves had turned brown or red. I even thought I detected a slight whiff of woodsmoke, which made me secretly happy even though I knew I would have to report it.

The Retreat House was right on the edge of the street, and some effort had been made to keep the ancient sidewalk in reasonable repair. I climbed the steps to the double front doors and entered.

The lobby, and, in fact, the entire facility, was clean and homey. There was no sign that it was really a combination of retirement home, convalescent home, and hospice, except perhaps for the faint scent of old age and disinfectant in the air. Some would say the Franklyns kept it so pleasant out of self interest. The servants who visited relatives were also likely to spend their own last years there, and might become discontent if the place wasn't attractive.

My father's rooms were impressive. While many of the retired servants' quarters were comfortable but spartan—like the quarters they had lived in during their working lives—my father's rooms reflected the life he had become accustomed to as manager of the Franklyn estate.

He had been an important man in my youth. A servant, but the most prominent servant. Our family had lived in a fine dwelling, not far from the main house, and the entire staff had treated my father with the same respect they gave to the holder's family.

He had a whole floor of the retreat house to himself and his staff. But as his health declined he mostly limited himself to a single large room, the only one with a fireplace—a testament to how highly the Franklyns esteemed him. It was monk-built, of course, powered by the Spirit. In spite of his status, he was not a holder, and not allowed a real fire.

The healer was leaving the room as I came in, and caught my eye. He gave a slight shake of his head to indicate that I wasn't to expect too much.

My father sat in front of the fire, staring into the flames.

I sat in the chair next to him, and waited for him to notice me. There was no trace of disinfectant in the air in this room, only fresh coffee, furniture polish, and the faint illusion of woodsmoke from the monkish flames. Finally he turned. He stared for a moment, then his eyes focused.

"Adam?"

"It's me, Dad."

His eyes dropped to my reversed collar.

"A costume party?"

"It's my vocation, Dad. I'm a pastor now."

He nodded, vaguely. I wasn't sure whether it was his illness, or whether he was pulling my leg. Quite possibly it was a bit of both.

My father had had a wicked sense of humor in his private life. It sometimes still came through. I knew he had been disappointed when I went off to seminary to train for ministry. He never said so out loud, and I never asked why. I suspected that he had wanted me to inherit his position as manager.

"So," he said, "not a costume." And I saw the tell-tale wrinkles at the corners of his eyes.

I laughed. "Not a costume. How have you been feeling?"

"Physically, fine . . ."

He raised one eyebrow and fixed an eye on me.

" . . .far as I can remember."

"And emotionally?"

"Emotionally? Content. Frustrated. Anxious."

"Content?"

He nodded, his eyes wandering toward the crackling fire.

"Content. With life. Except memory plays tricks. Can't always think straight."

He looked back at me.

"I get confused. Frustrates me. Comes and goes. Quite suddenly."

"And the anxiety?"

"Still things I need to do, before . . ."

"Anything I can help you with?"

He stared at me in silence for a moment. Something shifted behind his eyes.

"If your mother asked you to do something, would you do it?"

"If Mom asked?"

"If the next time you saw her . . ."

"She's dead, Dad. Over a year now."

He stared at me, deep in thought.

"Dad?"

He nodded, then stood.

"A horrible host. Let me take that and get you some coffee."

He scooped my Bible out of my hands before I could object and crossed the room to the table that held his breakfast. He slid the Bible into a drawer there, closed it, filled two mugs with coffee, and ambled back, thrusting one of them into my hands.

He collapsed back into his chair and raised his mug toward the pencil sketch which stood on the table beside him. My dad had made that sketch himself as a young man. It caught her perfectly; he could have had a career as an artist.

"Your mother."

We clinked mugs and drank. He motioned me forward, and leaned close.

"Quietly," he whispered, "we can be heard."

"But . . ."

He put a finger to my lips.

"You've become a rule-follower, Adam."

I decided to humor him, and replied in the same whisper.

"A rule-follower?"

"Are you more loyal to your family or to your rulebook?"

"My rulebook? You mean the Word of God?"

"I need to know." He seemed frightened. "For your mother . . . For myself, and others, but mostly for your mother." He nodded to himself, then continued. "I wasn't sure, you see. But she thought . . . Made me promise . . . I haven't much time left before . . . Before I won't be able to . . ."

"Dad," I whispered, "what—"

He had a little fit of coughing. I had seen this before. He was getting agitated.

"If I asked you—if she asked you—to keep a secret, a secret your rules told you not to keep, would you do it?"

"She's dead, Dad. What kind of secret?"

His breathing was heavy, and he had frantic look about him.

"Can you promise me that? Promise you would keep it?"

"I think you should lie down for a bit, Dad. You're getting—"

He grabbed my wrist.

"Promise me!"

I had to calm him down.

———

THE SECOND PROMISE I made that day weighed even more heavily on me.

The Franklyn estate was a study in intimidation—especially the main house. Most people could not approach it without feeling small and unimportant by comparison—and inferior to whoever lived there. That was not a mistake. It was, in fact, the entire point.

I was aware of the effect, but immune to it. It's impossible to be overwhelmed by an immense lawn when you played tag on it as a child. Where the stranger saw wealth and power in the great halls, I only remembered some very clever hiding places.

My visit with my father had made me a bit nostalgic for those days, so I took the long way in, steering my chariot along the inside of the great brick wall and across toward the manager's house. A slight breeze moved across the lawn, scented with fresh mown grass. There was a still a bit of wild garden where we had played as children, between the lawn and the manager's house. I floated through it, along the shade-mottled path, breathing in the pines, and then, on a sudden impulse, veered between the shrubs to the place where we had seen the guardian angel.

Boyd and Bee and I had been hiding there from Sam and Laine and Ras—I think we were the infidels in that game, and they were the bounty hunters. As the three of us crouched in the bushes, peering breathlessly through the branches, the angel shimmered into existence, about fifty feet away.

Bee put her hand on my arm, and Boyd gave me an astonished glance.

It spoke to someone just out of our sight, and we couldn't make out the words. We watched, holding our breath, until the short conversation was over, and the angel shimmered once more and was gone.

We had no doubt who it had appeared to. Even if we'd never seen an angel before, we knew enough about them to know that they didn't appear to just anyone. The only person on the estate who was important enough to have a conversation with an angel was Boyd's father, the Holder.

This excited us, especially Boyd. Was it possible that Mr. Franklyn had his own guardian angel? And if he did, did that mean that Boyd would have one, too, when he grew up to be the holder?

So Boyd had dreams of eventual status. I don't know how it

affected Bee. But I—I quite suddenly felt an overwhelming need to understand that whole other part of my world. That may have been the moment which decided my vocation.

Later, when I attended seminary, I would come to view angels as commonplace, even mundane. But at that moment I was overcome by awe—awe, and a powerful curiosity.

I hovered for a second or two above the spot where we had hidden, remembering that time and others, then turned my chariot toward the main house.

Chapter 3

-Squatter proverb

Anna Franklyn, Boyd's mother, was in her bed—healers hovering nearby. She reached out to me, weakly, and her eyes twinkled as I took her hand.

"Thank you for coming, *Pastor* Kinde."

I squeezed her hand and let it go. Her brows knitted and she became more serious.

"Have you been to see your father?"

"Just this morning."

"And how is he?"

"Confused. He seems to think Mother is still alive."

"I'm sorry, Adam. He's such a dear man, and you are so like him. Not just your looks. Your whole manner, really. And your kindness."

"I wish I deserved that."

She chuckled weakly.

"And Lucky," she asked, "how is he doing?"

"Lucky as ever. I think he may have a girlfriend. He's been spending a lot of evenings out lately."

"Really? Lucky?"

I nodded. "And how are *you* feeling, Anna?"

"I'm in need of some private counseling."

She looked pointedly at one of the healers. He nodded, then motioned to the others. They followed him out of the room.

She waited until she heard the latch click, then patted the bed by her side. I sat on the edge.

"I need your help, Adam. You're the only one I can turn to."

"What can I do?"

"I'm ready to die. More than ready. I thought I had it done, then they brought in this damned Lazarus Stone, and dragged me back again."

"You'd reject a miracle?"

"You would too, if you were in as much pain as I am. And . . ." She paused. "There are other reasons."

"But surely you can see that when God sends us a trial . . ."

"God didn't send this trial, humans did. You know full well that this is a common miracle, not a divine intervention."

She raised herself, painfully, on one elbow to look me in the eye.

"This was decided by human beings, for human purposes. It does me nothing but harm. It does Boyd nothing but harm, though he won't admit that."

I wasn't surprised that she knew the difference between a common miracle and an intervention. The distinction was ecclesiastical, part of the training for clergy that wasn't supposed to be shared with lay people. But in my experience senior holders often knew way more than they were supposed to.

"If you're asking me to intervene," I said, "I'm afraid I don't have any influence with the healing ministries. Are you sure they did this without your permission?"

"Absolutely. I made that perfectly clear. You can ask Boyd."

"Then why would they . . . ?"

"I think I know, but that's not the point. The point is I'm done, and I want it to stop."

I considered.

"I suppose I could register a complaint on your behalf with the Presbytery. I'm not entirely sure if . . ."

"That would take too long. What I want you to do is help me cheat them. I want you to figure out a way to get this damn thing out of the room without them realizing. And keep it out, until I'm gone."

"You're asking me to help you commit suicide."

"I'm asking you to let God's will take its natural course."

I sat up a bit straighter.

"It's my duty as your pastor to warn you against this sin."

"It may or may not be a sin, Adam. It's what I need, and need quickly."

"You realize you're asking me to commit murder, as well?"

"God damn it! It wouldn't be murder. I would be dead now if things had taken their natural course. It's this stone that's not natural. Adam, you know what I have done for your family, for you, over the years. I'm asking you to help me now, in my greatest need."

She collapsed back on her pillow from the effort of that speech, and lay there, staring at the ceiling.

I reached out to take her hand, but she yanked it away.

After a time she met my eyes again and spoke softly.

"Please, Adam. Please? Will you at least *consider* it?"

WHEN I CAME DOWNSTAIRS the butler told me that Boyd would want to see me and showed me into the library. Squatters, and most tenants, wouldn't even know what the word "library" meant, but it was still a traditional room in some holders' houses.

Boyd's library was inherited from his father, who had been a collector. It contained several shelves of books—all vetted by the church, of course. Even so he wasn't allowed to remove them from the room.

He had let me handle one once. It was a curious thing, a remnant of the Dark Age. Hundreds of rectangular pieces of paper—like the ones in my father's sketchpad, but white and smaller, maybe six inches by eight or ten—stacked together and attached at one of their long edges, protected on three sides by a more rigid paper, so that only the edges of the papers were exposed when the book was closed. Each of the papers inside had writing on them—the same as in my own Bible, except it was permanent. The writing never changed. To see the next bit you had to turn the paper over.

He told me that the thickest book in his collection only contained about 400,000 words. The scriptures are twice that size. The commentaries, theologies, and other texts I can read on my Bible would probably fill all the empty shelves in his library and more. No wonder it was built so large.

Boyd only used one small corner of the room—as a quiet place to do business tasks on his own Bible, which lay on a small table by his favorite chair.

He was nowhere in sight.

Like most puzzles—which meant anything I didn't yet understand—the contents of Boyd's Bible piqued my curiosity. I would have loved to know what Boyd's Bible contained that mine didn't. He probably would have felt the same way about mine.

But the chosen didn't share Bibles.

It was both illegal and a sin to show your open Bible to another if you were one of the chosen, or to try to see another's Bible. And of course his Bible wouldn't have opened for me, anyway.

But it didn't stop me from wishing it would.

The room was silent. Late morning light streamed from the leaded windows across the floor to the fireplace, which was empty. The logs were laid, of course, waiting to be lit, but Boyd hardly ever bothered with a fire for just himself.

I browsed the titles in his bookcase until he came striding in.

He clapped me on the shoulder.

"Adam! Did you come to see my mother?"

He was a large man, with a deep voice and a tightly trimmed beard. It was odd that I still saw my childhood friend in him, but I did.

"I just came from her room."

"Did she complain about staying alive?"

"I *am* her pastor."

He laughed and dropped into a chair, motioning me to do the same.

"Meaning you're not going to tell me anything. How's your father, or are you *his* pastor too?"

"He's as well as can be expected. Has trouble remembering Mom is dead. Can I ask *you* something about your mother?"

He stroked his beard and grinned.

"I *am* her son, you know."

"Yeah. Seriously, though."

"Ask away."

"Did she agree to the Lazarus Stone?"

"Oh. That. She wasn't in any shape to agree or disagree when they brought it in. She had told me some time before that she didn't want any miracles performed, but when the moment came I wasn't consulted. I'm not sure I would have been heeded, either. The healers were pretty determined. And, once it was done . . ."

He shrugged, then continued.

"I suppose she blames me?"

I shook my head.

"I don't think so. I can't say more."

He nodded.

"In that case, there's another matter I need to bother you with. I hope you won't take any offense, but I'm the one who'll have to be mysterious this time."

"Mysterious?"

"I need to ask you a rather insulting question, and I can't explain why. Let me put it the least insulting way I can: Am I right in thinking that you would never deal in unreported contraband?"

I was speechless. He laughed.

"I warned you it would be insulting. But I do need you to confirm it."

"Yes. I mean, you're right. I wouldn't."

He leaned forward, and the smile vanished from his face. My childhood friend was completely gone, and the holder was in his place.

"I wouldn't tolerate you lying to me, Adam."

I felt a chill go through me, then anger. My jaw tightened. I made myself meet his gaze.

"If you don't know me better than that . . ."

"Do you have any idea why someone might think you *are* in possession of something illegal?"

I was in no mood to even consider that.

"Are you sure they've got the right person?"

He relaxed a bit and leaned back in his chair.

"Don't let it worry you. Whatever it is, it's more about me than you."

He flashed his famous smile.

"That should keep your inquisitive mind busy for a day or two."

MY PARENTS WERE THRILLED the moment my name appeared on my Bible. I was only three or four years old when it happened. I was happy about it, too, but mostly because it made me more like Boyd. Most holders and tenants were chosen, so it was no big thing for him, but I was the son of a servant. I might never have been chosen at all.

So my parents were relieved that I wouldn't live out my life as a menial servant, never being trained by my Bible to read or write or understand math, never having access to a world of words, being destined to live on the level of a squatter, with a Bible that only spoke to me in pictures and stories.

And they were happy for another, private, reason.

I was just glad that the gap between me and my best friend had closed a bit.

And I also simply loved the process. I took to the word games immediately, and never noticed that there were fewer and fewer pictures and picture stories. I was proud of my new status, of the fact that only I was now allowed to view my Bible, that it was a Bible like my father's and like Boyd's, private and special.

Even as an adult and a pastor, visiting my father that day, I had no idea how important that moment had been.

THE QUARTET CONTINUED their medley as I watched her tug at that fingernail.

"The angels call to me,
Afar from heaven's door"

The nail came off the end of her finger and hung from a thin layer of skin. She tugged at the next one, and it did the same.

She was wearing the latest monkish fashion in gloves: "Miracle Skin", complete with "Miracle Nails". I hadn't anticipated that, probably because there was nothing else faddish about her.

I knew about Miracle Skin. I wasn't completely obtuse. I just pretty much ignored such things. I wore the current style for clergy, of course: the fedora and clerical collar, but that had been in style at least a decade. On the other hand, I didn't carry a walking stick, even though most men of my age and station did that year. It was a throwback to our parent's generation, and I didn't expect it to last. I tended to ignore the passing fads.

Miracle skin was almost certainly a passing fad. It was a very exclusive fashion, and the fact that she wore it was enough by itself to prove she was a holder, but I had already guessed what else I would see once they were completely off.

Her logo was on the back of her right hand.

So she *was* a holder—but only by relation. Unmarried, with access to lots of money, but no real power. She couldn't flaunt her status by not wearing a logo at all, but she could wear it on her hand instead of her forehead. And the introduction of miracle skin gloves made it possible to complete the illusion in public.

The mystery was solved. I could get back to my sermon.

But that was easier said than done with three problems bearing down on my mind. The difficulty was that I always kept my promises, and so usually avoided making them. But the ones I had made this morning were troubling.

I didn't know what secret my father had been referring to, and so had no idea what I might have taken on there.

And though I had only promised Anna to *think* about her request, I felt the obligation went beyond that, somehow. She had been a second mother to me. What she asked was impossible, of course. Putting aside the moral issue, I couldn't think of any way I could smuggle a Lazarus Stone out of her room without the healers noticing. Unless . . .

I stopped myself.

It was wrong, and that was the end of the matter. So how did I keep my promise to *consider* it?

And the third thing. What was the third thing? I couldn't remember at first, and then I did—that one had been solved already. She was a holder relation, and wore her logo on her hand. So there were really only two . . .

"Excuse me."

She was standing across the table from me, her hand—the one with the logo—on the back of the other chair.

She smiled. Again.

"Pastor Kinde?"

Chapter 4

"I witnessed an execution in the public square today. I would have avoided it had I known in advance. It was the first in our village. It clearly won't be the last."

Richard Kinde (ancestor of Adam Kinde)

I STOPPED on the way home at the police station, and asked for Detective Troy at the front desk. I didn't know the young desk sergeant, so I had to wait.

I sat on the bench against the wall while Dennis was being found and told that I was there. The bench had once been green. A fly buzzed against the window pane.

A few minutes later Dennis opened an interior door, and motioned me in. We wandered down silent halls, between walls that had also once been green, toward his office. At one turn I heard distant arguing behind closed doors, but couldn't make out the words.

Dennis glanced toward the sound and shrugged.

"We've got a hearing going on. A squatter. Caught selling her favors for water."

He opened the door to his office and motioned me to the chair on the other side of his desk.

He was a few years older than me and a couple of inches shorter, with the little paunch of a family man, prematurely silver hair which looked even whiter in contrast to his dark skin, and a head as round as a cantaloupe. He had constant furrow between his eyes, as though he couldn't believe what he was looking at. Sometimes it fit his sense of humor. Most of the time it made you think he was worried about something. He was an active member of my congregation—one of the steady people you could count on to show up to meetings and then to actually follow through. He was also a friend of sorts, constantly concerned about my unmarried state.

He slumped into his own chair with a weary sigh.

"You want some coffee? I don't recommend it."

"No thanks. I just came in to report a probable violation."

"Probable?"

"Well, almost certain. I didn't actually see it."

He nodded, then picked up his Bible and stylus.

"Time?"

"Early this morning. Maybe six-thirty or seven."

"Place?"

"Near the Lindley Retreat House."

"What didn't you actually **see** there?"

I laughed.

"I smelled woodsmoke."

He added the note.

"That's it?"

"That's it."

He shoved his Bible back on a shelf, next to a chipped

coffee mug and the iron rod which he refused to carry, then turned his attention back to me.

"We should have lunch sometime."

"We did, last Monday, remember?"

"That was the pastor and a board member, doing church business. I'm saying just you and me. People. Friends. We haven't done that in a couple of months."

"I'd like that."

"So how about next Tuesday?"

"Sounds good."

He stared at me in silence for a moment, then made a decision.

"You're not in any kind of trouble, are you?"

"Not that I know of. Why?"

"Nothing you want to tell me? Because if there is, it would be a good idea."

"I've had a little trouble with this weeks shipment of contraband, but aside from that . . ."

He sat up straight.

"Contraband? What kind?"

"That was irony, Dennis. A joke. I don't have any contraband, or any other problems that could involve the police."

I didn't mention Anna's request.

Dennis looked puzzled.

"So why 'contraband,' specifically?"

"What do you mean?"

"I ask you about trouble in general, and you bring up 'contraband'. Why?"

"I don't know, Dennis. It just popped into my . . . No. Actually I *do* know why. I had a chat with Boyd Franklyn this morning, and he asked me if I had any contraband. That was the word he used. 'Contraband'. I guess it just stuck in my mind."

"And you told him you didn't."

"Yeah. What's this all about?"

He considered.

"I suppose that would explain it."

"Explain what, Dennis?"

He sighed again.

"Why you mentioned contraband. And you don't have any, right?"

"Right."

"And you're *sure*?"

THE HEARING for the squatter woman was over. They were dragging her down the hall ahead of me as I left, out the front door and across to the public square. She dragged her feet, struggled against the officers, and finally went completely limp, so they had to carry her.

I usually avoided public executions, but for some reason this time I found it hard to tear myself away.

I stepped into my chariot, and floated toward the road home, but slowly enough that I witnessed the entire process. They pulled her to the center of the square and fastened her wrists into the iron cuffs. The cuffs were fastened to chains, with the other ends anchored in the ground so that she couldn't run.

The officers stood back, and the local executioner stepped forward, his Bible in one hand and his rod of iron in the other.

The few criminals I had seen executed before had all fallen to the ground, screaming and begging to be spared. But this woman stood, facing her death with something like defiance in her eyes.

The executioner lifted his Bible and called out the set formula in a clear and deep voice.

"Lucy Ford, do you confess to the act you have been charged with?"

The woman did not blink.

"I do."

"And do you ask for God's forgiveness for this sin?"

"I do not."

The executioner paused, a puzzled look on his face. He abandoned the usual order of questioning.

"You realize that this is your last chance to repent?"

"Yes."

"And you have already confessed to the sin."

"I have not."

"Don't waste our time. You did. Not seconds ago."

"I confessed to the *act*."

"I'm not here to play word games. I'm giving you one last chance to repent before your death. Do you repent?"

"I have nothing to repent of. Should I have let my family starve? My children die of thirst?"

There was a trace of disdain in her voice, and the executioner heard it. He lifted his iron rod and returned to the formula.

"I have given you the chance to repent, and you have rejected it. Let all who hear be witnesses."

Then he pointed the rod at her, and uttered the final curse.

The tip of the rod glowed blue for a moment, then the woman began to moan. Her moan grew into a scream, and then an unearthly wailing just before she burst into flames. I could feel the heat from the road. Within seconds there was nothing left of her. The iron cuffs lay on the ground empty.

As I turned to leave I saw Dennis, standing in the open doorway of the police station. He nodded toward the square, with something like a warning in his eyes.

I ARRIVED home a bit off-balance from the odd events of the day.

The parsonage was a very old building, added to the church property sometime in the late Dark Age, but well-maintained by an unbroken chain of pastors since. It was built of brick and plaster, with thick wooden beams, which had aged to a dark brown. The previous pastor told me it was a sort of fad in the Dark Age, called "Tudor". The house wasn't actually connected to the church proper like some of my colleagues' houses, so it had its own alter, and I had to invoke the Spirit once a week to keep the lights on.

We had three rooms downstairs: a living room just large enough for the occasional party with members of the congregation, a smaller room I used for the most private of counseling sessions, and the kitchen which more or less belonged to Lucky, the sole member of my staff.

The bathroom was upstairs, between the bedrooms. I took the smaller bedroom because I had an office to myself—also upstairs—and the entire property was properly my domain. I thought Lucky should have some space that was completely his own.

I inherited Lucky when my father retired. The new manager had wanted his own people, so Lucky had to go somewhere. I had just been ordained, so I took him on as cook, handyman, and general factotum. He had been a key figure in my father's staff for most of my life, and a bit of a second father to me.

In fact, I was the reason my father took him on in the first place.

I was barely a toddler, so I don't remember most of this, but the story is that my father had taken us into the city with him on estate business. He had dropped my mother off at the monastery shop while he attended a meeting. She had let me stand by myself for a moment while she tried on a pair of shoes, and a strange woman dragged me off when she looked away.

My mother saw her leaving with me and chased her outside, screaming for the woman to stop. But she got caught up in the crowd on the sidewalk and lost sight of us. A skinny young squatter—twenty-two or twenty-three—saw what was happening, yelled, "I'll follow her, lady! Get the police!" and disappeared on a dead run.

By the time my mother found a policeman, the squatter was back, grinning from ear to ear and carrying me. He had tracked the woman for several blocks, where she met up with a man in an alley. She had put me down, holding me by my collar with one hand, and the man was handing her some money when the young fellow swooped by, grabbing me on the run, and disappeared back into the crowd.

The police assumed that the two had mistaken my parents for holders and the man would have demanded ransom. They never knew for sure.

Lucky was that young squatter. His real name was Das. My grateful father gave him a position, and that was the beginning of his reputation for luck. His luck continued, and as often as not the payoff accrued to our household, so he rose in the ranks until he was a trusted adviser, even though he was not one of the chosen and couldn't read or do any but the most basic math. I secretly suspected that the luck was really a result of his quick reactions, innate intelligence, and street experience, but Das insisted that he was just incredibly lucky, so the myth— and eventually the nickname—persisted.

The kitchen was warm when I arrived home. Lucky was just pulling a batch of cookies from the oven. The cooling rack above the counter was lined with the loaves of bread he baked for the neighbors. He was in his mid-forties by then, still skinny, his sharp features framed by his thinning hair. The wrinkles around his eye—a trait he shared with my father—

betrayed his sense of humor, though I rarely saw an actual smile.

He put the tray down on the stove top.

"How's your father, Lad?"

"Pretty much the same. His mind wanders a bit."

"And Mrs. Franklyn?"

"She presented me with a . . . a difficult problem. I want to talk it over with you later."

There are few smells that can compete with the aroma of fresh baked cookies. I sampled one, from the stack on the table.

"You have perfect timing, Lucky. I've got a guest coming by after the service. Just tea and cookies—we'll eat late tonight. A new member of the congregation."

He eyed me thoughtfully.

"Holder, Tenant, or Squatter?"

"Does it matter?"

He watched me a second longer, then nodded.

"Holder, then. I'll use the good plates."

"The good plates will be fine. I'm going to go freshen up. Her name is Beth, Beth Raven. If she gets here before I'm back make her comfortable."

He looked surprised, then amused.

"Beth Raven?"

"Yes. Why?"

"And she's new to the congregation?"

"I'm in a hurry. What's the problem?"

"Nothing at all, Lad. A *young* woman then?"

"She asked for an appointment. She probably needs spiritual counseling."

"I'll set things up in the living room."

Chapter 5

"The Second Enlightenment—extending roughly from Descartes to the anti-clockwork laws of the late twenty-first century—was not a separate period, but was concurrent with the tail end of the the Long Domination. This was the period called 'the dark age' during the short domination."

Lois Bradford, *An Introduction to the Second Enlightenment*

I CONSIDERED PRAYING ABOUT ANNA.

At that point in my life prayer—except, of course, wordless prayer—was like having a conversation with God. I don't mean that I heard some deep voice instructing me or anything like that. But even though my own voice was the only one in my head, I definitely felt someone listening on the other end.

More than that, I would find my own perspective shifting under the weight of that listening presence. From the time I was a teenager, when Pastor Dean first taught me to pray, I found it impossible to lie while praying. I don't just mean that I avoided it on the theory that God was all-knowing. It was deeper than that. I couldn't have done it, even on purpose as some kind of experiment.

Over the years it became harder and harder to even deceive myself when I was in prayer. I would begin by unburdening myself about some current problem or concern, my head full of all the things I wanted to believe—about the facts, about the intentions of others, about the purity of my own motives. But as I explained the situation to that silent presence I would find myself questioning all of those assumptions. And by the time I was through my entire perspective would have changed.

All of this accomplished without God uttering a single word.

But I didn't need to pray about this one. I already knew why I was tempted, and I already knew that it wasn't just my affection for the old lady or my sympathy for her plight.

She had presented me with an unsolved puzzle and had offered me the chance to be a hero. Adam Kinde was supposed to swoop in on his white horse of intellectual superiority, outwit the guardians of her health, and save the lady from a fate worse than death.

All very tempting, but the "fate worse than death" was life itself, and the "rescue" would make *me* a murderer and *her* a suicide.

It wasn't a good sign that a church official was attending a Thursday evening service.

Weekday services were for the squatters. If a church official was going to make a friendly visit he would come on a Sunday, when the tenants and holders came.

So when I saw him standing at the back of the sanctuary, I knew he hadn't come for the sermon.

I understand there was a time, before the Millennium and the second coming of Joshua, when a weekly sermon was the center of a pastor's ministry—the single most important educational tool of the church.

I can't imagine the pressure that put on a minister. By the time I was a young pastor those days were ancient history, and the sermon was a vestige of another age—another dispensation. I still was required to produce one every week, but instead of preaching it once, on Sunday, I had to preach it six evenings as well, each time to a different segment of my congregation.

And they neither needed or appreciated my efforts. Their chief form of entertainment was also their chief source of education—the Bibles which they brought with them to the service. They had no need to be instructed in the faith by me.

The real reason they came to the service was for the imbuing of those Bibles with the Spirit. All of the singing of hymns, the reading of verses, and the sermonizing were merely window dressing.

I had no illusions. If the Word of God did not require the weekly blessing of the pastor on the altar of the church in order to continue supplying them with light and heat and spiritual education, not one in a hundred would darken the church's door.

My sermon was simply the price they had to pay.

But none of that explained the figure listening at the back of the sanctuary.

ONE OF MY seminary classmates composed a limerick:

"His glass was the size of a stein,

> *That officious old fellow named Brine,*
> *His preference was red,*
> *And that's why, it is said,*
> *That his face was the color of wine."*

It wasn't the cleverest poem I ever heard, but it captured the two essential facts—from an undergraduate point of view—about Presbyter Brine. He loved to drink, and his face betrayed the fact.

He was a beefy man, with a purple face and an overblown sense of his own importance. Unfortunately, he actually had some real importance in my small corner of the church.

He was, among other things, an ecclesiastical judge. I had first met him in that capacity—when I was in the under-school at the seminary. He had officiated at the inquiry into the death of one of my friends. His behavior on that occasion had left me with a permanent distaste for him.

He waited until the last squatter had gone. Clearly, he did not want to be overheard. The walk from the back of the sanctuary to the alter appeared to exhaust him. He was breathing heavily as he approached.

"Pastor, ahhh, Pastor Kinde. I'd like a word with you, if I may."

That "ahhh" was a little quirk of his. It had inspired several drinking games among the students at seminary. I always thought that was ironic.

I gestured toward the front pew.

"Of course. Shall we sit?"

"Good idea. I, ahhh, I need to ask you a rather serious question."

"A question?"

"You're a good man, Kinde. I always thought you would go far one day."

"Thank you, sir."

"Excellent sermon, that, by the way."

I was starting to get worried.

"I'm glad you liked it, sir."

"Yes. Well done. A man with your abilities—such a man needs to be *careful*, if you understand my meaning."

"Careful?"

"Yes. Careful."

The conversation didn't seem to be getting anywhere. I decided I would have to help it along.

"You wanted to ask me something?"

"It wouldn't do, you see, to, ahhh, to make any *mistakes* at this point in your career."

"Perhaps if you told me what mistake, exactly, you're warning me about . . ."

He blinked several times.

"It wouldn't do, for example, to be caught holding any illegal, ahhh, *objects*, if you see what I mean."

"Objects?"

"And if you were to, to *find* yourself in possession of anything like that . . . Well. The best thing to do would be to quietly—quietly, mind you—hand it over to someone who could protect you from the, ahhh, the *professional* consequences."

He blinked at me for a quiet moment, then spoke again.

"Well?"

"I'm afraid I don't understand, sir."

"Understand? It's simple enough. Will you or won't you?"

"Do what?"

"Hand the stuff over. Over to *me, now*?"

This had all the marks of a no-win scenario. I took a deep breath.

"I'm sorry, sir, but I really have no idea what you're talking about."

He quite suddenly stopped blinking. He fixed me with a steady penetrating gaze and nodded almost imperceptibly.

"Well, I gave you your chance. You can't say you weren't warned."

"Warned?" I said.

But he was already heaving himself to his feet. He stomped off down the aisle to the main entrance and was gone.

WHEN I GOT BACK to the parsonage my guest was already seated in the living room with a cup of tea in her hand. Lucky was standing across from her. They were laughing together like old friends.

When they saw me they exchanged a quick glance and stopped laughing.

She had changed into a simple white blouse since we had parted at The Humble Monk, and wasn't wearing her gloves. She had also gotten rid of the excess makeup. Her eyes twinkled.

"Pastor Kinde. I hope I wasn't too early. Lucky has been entertaining me until you could get here."

Lucky nodded, those giveaway crinkles in the corners of his eyes, and took himself out of the room.

Beth reached for the teapot.

"May I pour you a cup?"

I could see the Raven logo clearly on the back of her hand. I thought it was no wonder I hadn't recognized her at the restaurant. The Raven corporation was one of the smallest, centered in North Dakota, half a continent away.

I took the seat across from her, on the other side of the coffee table.

"Have you been waiting long?"

"It certainly didn't seem like long."

"I hope Lucky hasn't been entertaining you with any of his questionable stories."

She laughed.

"What a strange thing to hope. Is something wrong?"

"Why?"

"You looked a little worried when you came in."

"Oh, that. Just church politics."

I changed the subject.

"So what brings you to our little community?"

"I came here to visit you."

"In my capacity as a pastor, or . . .?"

"In your capacity as a son, still grieving for his mother . . ."

I was taken aback.

"Really, Miss Raven—"

" . . . as a young man who is just starting his career . . ."

"I must—don't you think that's a bit—"

" . . .and as someone who could use a friend."

I regathered my composure, and tried to wrest control of the conversation back.

"That's all very kind, Miss. Raven, but we only met today."

She smiled.

"A friend," she added, "who has *also* been an infidel and has also spied upon an angel."

That stopped me.

I put my tea down and squinted at her face. It took a moment before I could see what I was looking for.

"Bee?"

She nodded.

I grinned.

"The day we saw the angel. You remember that?"

She nodded again.

"Lucky recognized you," I said, "didn't he?"

"He recognized my name, at least."

"I think I only ever called you 'Bee'. I'm—I'm sorry I didn't..."

"Don't be. It was actually quite a compliment."

I HAD trouble getting to sleep that night. My head was too full of questions.

I couldn't figure out why everyone seemed to think I was in possession of some kind of contraband, or why it should be important to so many different people. What was the connection between Presbyter Brine, Boyd, and the police? What was it, exactly, they all thought I had? Why did they think I had it?

I loved a puzzle, but I hated an unsolvable puzzle. I needed more information.

I also needed to figure out what I was going to do about Anna. I'd been resisting the urge to pray about her—although admitting that was a bit of a prayer in itself.

And my father—was this promise he asked anything real at all, or just the ramblings of an old mind, a mind that thought my mother was still alive?

In the midst of all that was Bee. Why had she suddenly decided to look me up after all these years? I was glad she did, and that bothered me. Why was I so glad?

I forced myself to consider this list rationally.

I couldn't do anything about my father at the moment, or about Bee, or the whole question of contraband. The only thing I could actually make progress on was Anna.

I could stop avoiding the issue and force myself to pray about it.

Having made up my mind on that point, I promptly fell asleep.

I was awakened by a sound downstairs. Lucky was in the kitchen. Probably getting himself a late night snack.

I considered joining him. There were things from the previous day I wouldn't mind talking over.

As I listened, he left the kitchen and moved around the living room. So he wasn't getting a snack. Probably looking for something.

I rolled over and tried to get back to sleep.

I heard him coming up the stairs, and entering my office. Just as well I hadn't got up. But what could he be looking for in there?

It was just enough of a puzzle to keep me awake. I rolled over and listened. He moved around, opening and shutting drawers, so it must have been something small, but why the middle of the night?

What if it wasn't Lucky?

I swung out of bed, grabbed my robe from the chair , and was halfway to my door when I heard footsteps on the stairs again, going down this time.

By the time I opened my door, Lucky was coming down the hall from his room and my suspicions were confirmed. He nodded to me as he passed on the way to the stairs.

"Someone's in the house."

I followed.

The kitchen door slammed behind the intruder, and by the time we got downstairs there was no one in sight.

Chapter 6

"The interactions of enlightenment and domination during this mixed period were often complex and unpredictable. New knowledge and technology fueled by the Second Enlightenment made possible the Industrial Revolution—a tool of domination. Struggles between the rich and powerful created windows of opportunity for the masses. Tools designed to increase communication and knowledge were used to spread disinformation."

Lois Bradford, *An Introduction to the Second Enlightenment*

"YOU'RE ABSOLUTELY certain nothing is missing?"

Dennis Troy stood in the kitchen, staring morosely at the broken window in the door to the street.

I shrugged.

"As near as we can tell. Certainly nothing valuable."

"And he was all over the house?"

"He or she. The kitchen, obviously. And I heard someone poking around the living room. I thought it was Lucky—and Lucky thought it was me, at first. Then I heard footsteps on the stairs, and someone opening drawers in my office. So those three rooms."

"And you think he was looking for something small?"

"Small enough to fit in a drawer, anyway."

Dennis nodded.

"There's not much we can do. Since we don't know what he took, or even *if* he took anything, there's nothing to trace. I'd put someone outside for a couple of nights, but I don't see the point. He either got what he wanted or discovered it wasn't here."

"So it's okay to clean up and fix the window?"

"Yeah. Just . . . you're *sure* you don't know what he was looking for?"

I rolled my eyes.

"You mean 'contraband'?"

"If there's anything left for him to find, it might be worth watching the house, that's all. Even if I didn't know *officially*."

"Thanks, Dennis. But I really have no idea what that's all about. And it's not just you and Boyd. I was contacted by Presbyter Brine yesterday as well."

Another voice intruded.

"What happened here?"

It was Bee, standing just outside the broken window.

I swung the door open.

"We had a break-in last night. Be careful of the broken glass."

Dennis gave me a knowing look. I rolled my eyes again.

"Dennis, this is Beth Raven—an old friend who's visiting."

I turned back to Beth.

"Dennis is a friend, a member of the church board, and a police detective—in that order."

She smiled that equal smile and thrust out her hand.

"Hi, Dennis."

Dennis hesitated, a bit embarrassed, then shook it.

"Nice to meet you."

She turned her attention back to me.

"So Adam," she said, "does this mean you're canceling our breakfast date?"

"Are you going to do it?"

Bee's eyes sparkled with adventure.

"And can I help you?"

We had moved our breakfast plans to the Humble Monk. The National Gospel Quartet blared over the other conversations and the clatter of dishes.

I had received a message from my father's healer on my Bible during breakfast. He had taken a turn for the worse, so I was planning on visiting him as soon as we finished. When I filled Bee in on my father's condition, she insisted on coming with me. It was against my better judgment, but there was no dissuading her.

In an ill-conceived attempt to change the subject, I told her about Anna's bizarre request. It was indiscreet, and possibly dangerous, but I seemed to have lost all my reserve, blurting out all sorts of private information without thinking.

Far from being shocked, Bee thought Anna's request was both sensible and exciting.

"Can I help you?"

I buttered my toast.

"Of course I'm not going to do it. It would be murder, not to mention impossible."

She raised an eyebrow at me.

"Impossible? That just makes it more tempting."

"Yeah, well, 'tempting' is the operative word."

"Seriously, there must be a way, and if she wants it that badly . . ."

"There's really no point in talking about this. It would be murder. Even worse, since she asked for it, it would qualify as suicide on her part."

Bee contemplated the chunk of omelet on her fork.

"It might be relatively easy," she mused, "to get the stone out of the room. The trick would be how to keep the healers from noticing . . ."

"Can we change the subject?"

"Okay, tell me this. Why is suicide a sin?"

"That's not changing the subject."

"Sure it is. *Why*?"

"It's basic doctrine."

"Based on what?"

"Based on the Word of God."

"The scriptures?"

"Yes."

"Where?"

I considered.

"Thou shalt not kill."

She swallowed a mouthful of omelet.

"Seriously?"

"Killing is killing. It doesn't say 'Thou shalt not kill anyone but thyself'."

"Maybe not. But does it actually say, anywhere at all, that suicide is murder?"

I thought about that.

"I don't think so. Why would that matter?"

"It matters . . . because . . ."

She took another bite of her omelet and chewed thoughtfully, staring off into space. Finally, she swallowed and pointed at me with her fork.

"So, you have this word, 'murder,' and it names a sin, and you want to know what that sin includes, right?"

"For the sake of argument, I guess."

"So you look at the context."

"The context?"

"Yeah. For instance, what's the penalty?"

"For murder?"

"Yes."

"It's death. Capital punishment."

"And it says that in the scriptures?"

"Yes."

"And capital punishment is killing, right?"

"Well, yes. But—"

"So, if *all* killing were murder, capital punishment would be murder."

"I'm not sure that—"

"And, that would mean the death penalty for whoever executed the murderer, right?"

"Well, it would, *if*—"

"*And* for the person who executed the executor, and the person who executed the person who executed the executor, and so on. A real bloodbath."

"But capital punishment isn't the same thing."

"So not *all* killing is murder?"

"Right. There are exceptions."

"Does it say anywhere in the scriptures that capital punishment is an exception?"

"I don't think so."

"So how do you know it is?"

"Everything you just said. If it isn't an exception, it leads to an absurd conclusion."

She nodded at me over her coffee mug.

I was getting impatient.

"*This* is not a case of capital punishment."

She put her cup down, and smiled.

"You just said that capital punishment can't count as murder, because it leads to an absurd result—right?"

"Yes, but that's not the same as suicide."

"Wouldn't it be even more absurd to exact capital punishment for a suicide? To execute someone *after* they've taken their own life?"

She stuck another forkful of omelet into her mouth, and beamed at me triumphantly.

THE DIFFERENCE in my father was shocking.

The room was much the same as it had been the day before. The drapes were drawn, making the room a bit darker, but not much else had changed. Light flickered from the fireplace, the scent of furniture polish and coffee still permeated the air, a fresh breakfast had been laid out on a side table.

But my father was in his bed, and seemed to be having trouble breathing. It had only been a little over twenty-four hours, but he seemed a lot frailer than he had the last time I saw him.

He sensed me standing by the bed and opened his eyes. I thought I saw recognition there.

"Good morning, Dad."

"Adam."

"That's right. How are you feeling?"

His eyes managed to crinkle a bit. He wheezed as he spoke.

"Never better."

I nodded.

"I brought you a visitor, if you're up to it."

His eyes wandered past me and fixed on Bee. They crinkled again.

"A young woman. It's about time."

"No, Dad. This is Bee. Remember her? She's come for a visit."

He focused on her again, searching, as I had, for the child's face in the woman's features. At last he smiled.

"Well, Bee. Good of you to come."

He looked back at me.

"Congratulations, Son. You couldn't do better."

"No, Dad. It's not like that. Bee is just visiting, and she wanted to see you."

Bee chuckled.

"Oh, I agree with your father. You *couldn't* do better."

The two of them locked eyes, amused at my discomfort. I tried to think of a way to change the subject, but Bee spoke first.

"I was sorry to hear about Aunt Mary."

He nodded almost imperceptibly, and his eyes glistened. It was both sad and a relief. At least he knew that Mother was dead.

"Is there anything I can do for you, Dad? While I'm here?"

The old confusion entered his eyes, and I knew we were losing him again. He seemed to be struggling to remember something.

"You remember your promise, Adam?"

He made a weak gesture toward my hand—the one that held my Bible.

"I can't tell you the rest. Not right now. But don't . . . when I'm gone, don't be in a hurry to . . ."

He searched out Bee, and reached for her with a shaking hand. She stepped closer and took it in both of hers.

His eyes pleaded with her.

"Don't let him . . . let him do anything . . . until Mary . . . Mary tells him . . ."

"Dad. Mary—Mom. She's no longer— "

But Bee caught my eye and shook her head. She patted his hand.

"Don't worry. I'll make sure. He won't."

His sank back into the pillow, and the worry went out of his face.

"Promise?"

She smiled.

"I'll see to it."

Chapter 7

BEE WAS anxious to visit Anna, but Dennis had asked me to stop by the police station after breakfast, and I wanted to do that first. I needed to see if he had any new thoughts about the theft. I didn't entirely believe his theory that the thief wouldn't be back.

I wasn't very anxious to take Bee to see Anna, either. I was sure she really did want to visit the poor woman, and from the best of motives. But I was also afraid that she saw the visit as a chance to check out Anna's room and plot the theft of the Lazarus Stone.

Dennis was at the front desk, talking to the sergeant there, when we came in. He looked up and motioned me toward the inner door.

"She'll have to wait out here."

She took a seat on the once-green bench, and Dennis escorted me down the once-green hallway. But instead of taking me to his office he stopped at his boss's door.

The sign on the door read *Tho Gesed, Chief of Police*. Dennis knocked once, and a voice from inside responded.

"Come!"

The room was much larger than Dennis' office, and unlike Dennis' office some attempt had been made at decoration. There were framed paintings on the walls, and good ones, too —the kind you would be more likely to see in a holder's home. The desk was expansive and empty except for a Bible and an iron rod of the police variety. But where Dennis' empty desk looked barren, this desk was merely impressive.

Sitting behind it was Tho Gesed, "Papa Tho", as he was known by the locals. He was a big man in his late forties or early fifties, large rather than fat, with a roundish face that constantly beamed a fatherly smile. He didn't stand, but leaned over the desk and stuck out an enormous fleshy hand.

I extended my own, and his engulfed it with a firm shake.

"Welcome, Pastor! It's good to see you somewhere other than church!"

He glanced at Dennis.

"You can go, Detective."

Dennis retreated, and Tho leaned back in his tooled leather chair. It was the only chair in the room, so I had to remain standing.

He looked me over, still beaming that smile.

"I hear you've had a burglary, Pastor."

"A break-in, anyway. We didn't find anything missing. I can't even be sure it was a thief."

"What else would it be?"

"I don't know. He—or she—rifled through my desk drawers. Maybe snooping, rather than looking for something to steal. Or maybe they just didn't find whatever they were looking for."

He grinned even broader and shook his head.

"Have you been on the wrong side of the law before, Pastor?"

"Before?"

"Any run-ins with the police in your past?"

"I got taken in for drunk and disorderly once during my student days, but they just dumped me back at the seminary."

"Hmm. I could check that, so it's probably true."

He put his hands behind his head and swung his boots—fancy tooled leather things, like the chair—up on the corner of his desk.

"Now the question in my mind is whether you are just so good you never got caught, or whether this really is your first time."

"My first time?"

"It doesn't matter. Here's what we're going to do. I'm going to offer you a very generous deal. You see, Pastor, for reasons that you don't need to understand, I'd rather not see this whole thing become an official inquiry. So I guess you and I are on the same side as far as that's concerned. Follow me so far?"

"No."

He let out a belly laugh.

"If certain items show up on this desk in the next seventy-two hours, I'm going to take care of the whole problem without getting you involved. That okay with you?"

"Look. Chief. I really have no idea, at all, what you're talking about. If you could just tell me what it is you think that I have . . ."

He exploded with laughter then, shaking his head some more while his eyes caressed me like a lost son.

"Well, I'll give you this: first time or not, you're very, very, good."

His smile vanished.

"Son, if you know what's healthy for you, you'll cut the crap. Because if I don't see that stuff on this desk in the next three days, your life as you know it will be over."

He drew a finger across his throat, and then his smile was back as quickly as it had left.

"It's been nice chatting with you, Pastor. You can find your own way out. I'll look forward to seeing you soon."

<hr>

I lost all interest in talking to Dennis after that.

Bee wasn't on the bench when I came out. She'd left a message with the desk sergeant—she had started walking toward the Franklyn estate, and I could catch up with her when I was done.

It actually made sense. We had walked everywhere that morning, but the estate was at the other end of the Valley. My chariot would only hold two people if we stood very close to each other, and that would not look good in town. This way, by the time I walked home, got the chariot, and caught up with her we would be far from any tenant gossip.

On the other hand, she might already be entering squatter territory, an idea I didn't like at all.

So I hurried to the parsonage, got my chariot, and followed her, pausing only for the briefest exchange with Lucky.

I found her just outside of town. She was standing by the side of road, deep in conversation with a young man who had the slightly emaciated look common to squatters. His long hair was tied at the back of his head with a leather strap; other than that he wore only a sort of rough skirt which barely covered his thighs. As I slowed my chariot to a stop he glanced my way, gave me a polite salute, and strode off the road into the maze of squatter territory.

I watched him go as Bee stepped onto my chariot.

"Who was that?" I asked.

She laughed.

"Just a person who lives near here."

"A squatter."

"Yes."

"Do you know him?"

"I do now."

This wasn't getting us anywhere. I tried again.

"The thing is, you're not familiar with the Valley as an adult, I mean. You should probably be careful about talking to squatters around here. It might not be safe."

"You're worried about me."

"Well, yes. I am. I don't know what it's like where you live, but around here, anyway, squatters aren't . . . aren't . . ."

"Good people?"

"Some are. Of course. But you shouldn't just assume—"

"Aren't they members of your congregation?"

"Well, technically. The ones who live around here anyway."

"They come to worship once a week. They listen to your sermons."

"They have to—to get their Bibles blessed. I'm just saying that it's probably not entirely safe to assume that any squatter you happen to bump into can be trusted."

She gave me a long, penetrating look, then sighed.

"So how far is it to the estate?"

ANNA SHOOED the healers from her room, then held her arms out.

She had recognized Bee immediately.

"Oh my dear, you've grown up completely since I last saw you. Are you still fond of berries and milk?"

"I still am, Mrs. Franklyn."

"Call me Anna, dear. Is your mother doing well?"

"She's getting on. This visit was her idea, actually. She wasn't up to coming herself, so . . ."

Anna glanced in my direction.

"She's a wise woman, your mother. I wish Boyd were home. He would love to see you again. You must promise to drop by tomorrow."

"I promise. Adam was telling me about your problem, Mrs. Franklyn—"

"Call me Anna."

"Anna, then. Anyway, he was telling me about it, and I was thinking—"

I interrupted.

"She's the only one I've told, Anna. I'm sorry—it was indiscreet, I know, but . . ."

Anna put a hand on mine.

"I think she's safe enough. Just don't go blabbing it anywhere else."

She turned to Bee.

"So, dear, you were saying?"

THE POLICEMAN WOULDN'T LET me into my own house.

Bee and I had stopped the chariot just outside of town and walked the rest of the way while it followed. We had argued for most of the trip about Anna's request.

I finally dropped her off at the house she had rented, and turned the chariot toward home. I was frustrated. My head was jumping from one problem to another—the mysterious "contraband", my father's vague requests, Anna's problem, the break-in, and Bee.

Given my other problems, I was spending an inordinate amount of time thinking about Bee.

I wanted nothing more than to get home and either talk the whole mess over with Lucky or lock myself in my office in silence to think.

But there was a policeman standing in the doorway, and he wouldn't let me in. I didn't know him, though he was almost certainly a member of my congregation. He was a surly fellow with broad shoulders, and the second I began to rant and rage he pulled the rod from his belt. He looked like he would use it on me, too—clergy or not.

I finally calmed myself enough to take another tack. I asked if there was a superior officer on the premises.

"Yes, sir. There is. Detective Troy, sir. He's supervising the search."

"Could you please tell Dennis I'm here?"

The fellow considered that, then called over his shoulder into the house.

A few minutes later Dennis appeared.

"Sorry about this. Chief Tho's orders. We're to search the entire premises for your contraband."

"Can you tell this fellow to let me in?"

Dennis was clearly embarrassed.

"I can't. Orders. We're to keep you out until we're through. Also, we're to keep you here, now that you know we're searching. And we're going to have to search the sanctuary as well."

I sat down on the edge of the planter by the door. Apparently Tho had told me I had three days just to keep me from moving the "stuff" before he could do a search. Or maybe not. Maybe this was just another way to show me he meant business. I really didn't care anymore.

Dennis put a hand on my shoulder.

"I've threatened them with extra duty if they leave a mess."

I sighed.

"Okay, Dennis. But do me a favor. Make it a damn good search. If there's anything here, find it. I want this whole thing to be over and done with."

Dennis gave me a pained grin.

"Oh we'll find it if it's here. Never fear."

Chapter 8

<blockquote>

"He began his adventures trapped in the interplay of radically different roles: son of a servant, friend of holders, junior member of the clergy—he was friend and pastor to a policeman, and viewed his only servant as a childhood mentor."

</blockquote>

Silas Redford, *The Real Adam Kinde: An Experiment in Biography*

I WAS dead on my feet by the time I got home after services.

Dennis' search had turned up nothing, but had taken most of the afternoon. The evening service was delayed until his crew finished searching the sanctuary, and I waited outside in the twilight with the congregation until they let us in.

I doubt if anyone paid any attention to my sermon with an unexplained police search on their minds. I know I didn't. But it was Friday, and I had already preached the same homily to five other congregations, so I must have done it by rote. I couldn't have said for sure.

I was slower than usual straightening things up after the service, and by the time I left there was no one else in sight. The night was clear and dark, not quite a new moon. It was chilly, and I hurried home, ready for a warm supper and an early night, my way lit only by the statue of Joshua on the corner.

Lucky had roast lamb and potatoes ready, and the two of us ate it in silence. I would have liked to talk things over with him, but I was too tired.

After supper I climbed the stairs to my office, closed the door behind me, collapsed into my reading chair, and tried to think.

I woke sometime in the middle of the night, stiff from sleeping upright. I stretched my neck and rolled my shoulders and decided to go to bed.

But the sleep had taken the edge off, and I found myself sitting in the dark, running the events of the last two days through my mind.

The first priority had to be this business about the contraband. Bee was a pleasure (I had to admit) and a nuisance, and she could become a serious problem where Anna was concerned, but not immediately. Anna's demands were tricky, but in the end there was probably nothing real I could do about them. My father's ramblings quite possibly meant nothing at all.

I had to figure out what Tho and Presbyter Brine and Boyd thought I had, and how to convince them that I didn't have it.

Or find it.

The thought had popped into my head uninvited, but it made sense. What if there *was* something I had—something I didn't *know* I had? Something important enough for all those people to be interested in, something illegal.

That would explain the break-in. If someone knew—as apparently the entire world did—that I had this stuff and came looking for it...

It had to be small, because the intruder had gone through my desk. Smaller than a breadbox, then. But where could it be? Dennis' team had combed the house already. They had looked in every corner, and turned up nothing. So it would have to be somewhere they would never look.

And why wouldn't they have looked there?

Because they didn't know the place existed. That was the only possibility. There was a place in this house that maybe even I didn't know about.

And then I thought I did know.

It had bugged me from the day I moved in. One of those unsolved little mysteries that your brain just can't let go of. The upper floor of the parsonage was wider, by about six feet, than the lower floor. It was cantilevered out, forming a ceiling for the brick patio that ran along the back of the house.

The lower floor was only about sixteen feet wide, which would make the upper floor twenty-two feet wide. My office took up the entire right end. It only had windows at the back, overlooking the garden. But it didn't feel long enough. The problem had gnawed at my mind for weeks when I first moved in. Finally I had measured it. It was only twenty feet from front to back.

That also irritated me. Why would someone leave a dead space just two feet wide in a building like that?

I eventually convinced myself to stop thinking about it. The building had been built during the Dark Age, and one didn't expect any serious rationality from that period. But mostly, other problems—with more immediate implications—had driven it from my mind.

I stared at the wall, which was covered with a large built-in cabinet—part cupboards and part a wardrobe where I kept my preaching clothes.

Just possibly it wasn't dead space. I had pictured a narrow space with bare studs on both sides, empty except for dust, cobwebs, and perhaps some mouse droppings. But I could have been wrong.

I heaved my stiff body out of the chair and crossed to the cabinet.

I swung the doors to the wardrobe open and pushed the clothes to one side. The back panel seemed solid enough. But when I tapped on it, it sounded hollow. I pushed, but nothing gave. I felt around for a hidden latch, but found nothing.

I tapped again. It was definitely hollow.

I braced my feet with both hands on the panel and leaned into it, pushing hard.

There was a quiet snap. Something gave, and the entire panel retreated about an eighth of an inch.

It wouldn't go any farther, so I tried to push it sideways. It slid smoothly out of the way, revealing a narrow storage area. There were no cobwebs or mouse droppings, and the walls were finished off. The back wall, a little less than two feet away, was covered with bookshelves, similar to the ones in Boyd's library.

They were mostly empty, but there were a handful of books on the shelf directly in front of me. I recognized a couple of titles—books I could have accessed on my own Bible, given my status as clergy. *The Great Divorce*, by Jack Lewis, and *The God I Don't Believe In*, by Gary Wilburn. They were both studied in seminary as examples of how subtly heresy could infect the thinking of the righteous.

The rest of the books were written by authors I had never heard of: Vonnegut, Feynman, Whitman, Lao Tzu, Adams, and others.

So one mystery was solved.

I was tempted to look them over before turning them in. It took all of my self-control to resist that—but I knew it would be dangerous, not to mention wrong.

I inspected the latch which was holding the panel shut. The pastor who had owned this collection (it had to have been a pastor—the building had been a parsonage for generations) had not only collected illegal books. He had clearly dabbled in clockwork as well.

It was very cleverly designed, and it took me a while to figure out how it worked. When the panel was closed, you had to press on it near the latching mechanism while turning the rod the clothes hung on at the same time. This released the panel so it could move back and slide out of the way.

Unfortunately, I had broken it by pushing so hard. It would close, but felt loose to the touch. If the thief returned before I took the books to Tho, he might easily spot the hiding place.

I decided not to risk it. I pulled the books out, and took them to my desk. I moved most of the junk that had collected in the largest of my desk drawers into the others and crammed the books in there.

My burglar wasn't likely to waste his time searching the same place twice.

Chief Tho had given me three days, but he'd also had my house searched a few hours later. I had every reason to take the books in, explain how I found them, and get him off my back.

So why didn't I?

Partly it was timing, I suppose. I had already promised to take Bee to see Boyd after breakfast before I knew the books existed.

Partly it was relief. Now that I knew what I had, and that I had plenty of time to turn them in, it just didn't feel so urgent.

Partly it was because I had to decide who I was going to turn the books over to. Would Tho or Brine be the wiser choice? Since I had no idea why they wanted them so badly, I had no idea how to decide between them.

And even though I knew better, I was also a bit tempted to look through them first, just enough to see what all the fuss was about.

In any case, I didn't turn them in that morning, or even that day. Things might have turned out differently if I had.

Boyd was waiting for us in his library, the fireplace blazing for the sake of guests. He was genuinely glad to see Bee again, and for a couple of hours it was like old times. I hadn't realized how much of his ongoing friendship with me was tainted by our class difference. But having it completely disappear while the three of us shared memories from childhood was like entering a different world.

I wondered if he noticed as well.

Just as we were leaving, Boyd shifted our relationship back to the present. He asked if I had any more thoughts about "that matter we were discussing the other day."

I could have told him then about the books, and maybe that would have changed things, as well. Maybe I would have, if I hadn't just been made very conscious of the social distance between us. But instead I remembered Tho's threats, and Brine's, and that both of them wanted the whole matter kept quiet.

"If you mean the 'contraband,'" I said, "no. I don't."

Bee's ears pricked up.

"Contraband? What's all this?"

Boyd shook his head.

"Nothing."

"Come on boys, tell Mama everything."

Boyd glanced at me and pulled at his beard. I suppose he opened up then because Bee was a fellow holder.

"Another corporation is mounting a hostile takeover, trying to push me out of most of my holdings. I've been fighting them off for almost a year. It even looked like I had them beat about a month ago, but this week I was approached by someone I had considered an ally. He offered me his support—which I thought I already had—*if* I could get hold of some contraband for him. He wouldn't tell me what it was. Only that Adam had it."

He turned to me.

"But Adam knows nothing about it, so the whole thing's a mystery."

I think I was on the edge then. Our long morning had reminded me of childhood bonds. On the other hand, admitting that I had just lied about the books could have made Boyd question my loyalty forever. And I couldn't see how a handful of old volumes could possibly be that important. So part of me wanted to tell him, and part of me wanted to look those books over before doing anything else.

I don't know which way I would have jumped, because at that moment my Bible vibrated with a word for me.

My father was dying.

Chapter 9

"Understanding is the key to life, not rules. Rules are too often an attempt to control others, to avoid our better instincts, or to avoid the hard work of discernment. They can be useful, as rules of thumb—but they are not the laws of the universe. We are almost always capable of being wiser than our thumbs."

Jeffrey Kinde (father of Adam Kinde)

MY FATHER HAD ALWAYS inspired loyalty from his staff. All the years he served the Franklyn corporation, any one of them would have done anything he asked, and more, without question. Now I realized that he'd had the same effect on his healer, who stood at the other side of his bed almost as grief-stricken as I was.

When I arrived he was wheezing as he breathed, eyes closed, apparently not conscious. I took his hand and squeezed it, and he squeezed back, though without much force.

"Dad," I said, "it's me, Adam."

He stirred then, opening his eyes.

"Adam." He squeezed my hand again. "Remember your promise?"

I couldn't see the point of discussion.

"Yes, Dad. I remember."

"You'll keep it for me?"

"Of course."

His eyes moved to the healer, then back to me.

"Wait. For your mother to ask you. She'll ..."

"Okay, Dad. I'll wait."

His breathing labored then, and his grip on my hand tightened.

"... serious ..."

"Yes."

"... love ..."

"Me too."

And he was gone.

LUCKY TOOK the news almost as hard as I did. I don't think I had realized that my father had been a father figure to him as well, even though he was almost twenty years older than me.

Bee and Boyd had arrived shortly after my dad died. Boyd brought us home in his chariot, which seated six, mine following behind.

Bee sized up the situation, sent Boyd back to the estate, and took the two of us—Lucky and me—in hand. She listened to us, pumped us full of tea, listened some more, sat with us in silence, listened again, and held us as we cried. In the midst of all that, she arranged for the associate pastor from the nearest church to take my place for the Sunday morning service, made dinner, forced us to eat, washed the dishes, and cried a little herself.

When she sent us up to bed, I expected her to lock up and find her way home, but apparently she spent the night on the couch, because we woke the next morning to coffee brewing—with bacon, omelets, and toast on the kitchen table.

Lucky insisted on repairing the kitchen window after breakfast. I saw it as his way of dealing with his grief, so I didn't object. Bee and I moved to the living room with our coffee. We sat side by side on the couch, and she put a hand on my arm, like she had done all those years ago when we saw the angel.

"So tell me what else I can do to help."

"Nothing. At least nothing I can think of right now. I'll have to write the obituary. The funeral will have to be scheduled, but since I'm the pastor, that won't be a problem. Thank you for yesterday though, and breakfast."

She nodded, and we sat in silence for a few minutes, then I spoke again.

"I'm sorry I gave you such a hard time about Anna. It's just that I can't do what she wants, and I really don't know how to help her."

"I deserved it. You're her pastor. It's not my business what you should or shouldn't do. Same with your father. I shouldn't have jumped in there, either."

"You were completely right about that. Arguing was just agitating him. He made me promise again before he died, you know, but I followed your lead."

"And you still don't know what he wanted?"

"It was some delusion. He kept saying my mother would tell me. So . . ."

"You don't suppose it's related to that other thing? What you and Boyd were talking about?"

"That's something completely different. Actually, can you keep a secret?"

I took her upstairs to my office and filled her in on Presbyter Brine and Chief Tho and their threats. Then I showed her the books, and the secret space behind the cupboard.

"Two days ago the problem was just that everyone thought I had something I didn't have. Now I *do* have it, and I don't know which one to tell, or whether I should tell any of them. I don't know what I should do."

She studied my face.

"What you *should* do?"

"Yeah. The right thing to do."

"*The* right thing. You think there's only one?"

"I hope there's at least one."

"What do you *want* to do?"

"That's not the question."

"Humor me."

I narrowed my eyes.

"If I could do anything I wanted, without any consequences, I think I'd figure out how to fix that panel, put the books back where they were, and attend to my father's funeral. Then, when that was done, I'd read every one of them."

"And you can't do that, because . . ."

"Because I would be lying to a friend, because Tho would make my life hell, because Brine would probably have me defrocked and sent to a monastery."

"So there's a list of things you want. You want to read those books. You want to be a good friend to Boyd. You want to escape Tho's clutches. And you want to keep your pastorate."

I gave her a reluctant grin.

"I don't want much."

"Which of those four things do you want most?"

"You mean if I were to be totally selfish? I already told you —I'd like to fix that panel—"

She put up a hand.

"Different question. That was your answer if there were no consequences. But, as you just pointed out, there *are* consequences. I'm not asking you to imagine what some completely selfish version of you would want most. That person doesn't exist. I'm asking which of those four things you—the you who is here right now, who is *not* completely selfish and who understands those consequences—which of those four thingss *that* particular you wants the most."

"But that's not the point."

"Humor me."

"You already said that."

She just stared at me. I gave in and thought about it. And I was surprised.

"I want to be honest with Boyd."

She smiled.

"More than you want to avoid all the pain Tho and Brine can cause you?"

"I guess . . . Yes. I do."

"And more than you want to read those books?"

"Yes."

"Well, that doesn't solve your problem, but doesn't it simplify it?"

I WAS IN MY STUDY, the afternoon light streaming through the leaded window, writing my father's obituary when Lucky brought the boxes in. The Lindley Center had sent over my father's possessions. There were two boxes, and on top of them he placed my father's walking stick.

I had been fascinated by that stick as a child. I'd studied the way he carried it, the way he walked with it, the way he lifted it to gain a waiter's attention or leaned on it with both hands when explaining an important point to a subordinate, the way he pointed it at my chest when accusing me of some misdemeanor.

"And who, exactly, ate those cookies?" or,

"You, young man, have some explaining to do."

The walking stick was topped with a large knob of dark green stone, carved to resemble an elaborate spherical knot. My father had referred to it as a "Gordian Knot", and though he never explained the reason, he had told me many times that it was his reminder that knots should rarely be cut.

I could still see him, sitting on the stone bench just outside our front door on the Franklyn estate, turning the stick in front of me as he spoke. The light, dappled by the leaves of the old oak, reflected on the elaborate "knot". I could even smell the perfume from the roses at his back.

"Life is full of knots, son," he'd said. "And some people think it's wisdom to simply slash through them when they get in your way, not wasting your time or energy in unraveling them. But the gain in that is almost always an illusion. The person who relies on brute force to cut through the problems of life never learns the secrets hidden in the knots. What he gains in speed he loses in understanding, and understanding is almost always the more valuable of the two."

I leaned his walking stick against the wall and turned to the boxes.

The larger one contained clothing. I sorted through it quickly, and the only thing I wanted to keep was the cap he had worn, with the Franklyn logo, while running the estate. He had fastened his badge to it, the one that had identified him as the manager.

I hung it next to my fedora on the hat-rack by the door.

The other box was surprisingly small. My father had lived a large life, and there had been times when he and my mother would have left a great deal to be sorted out. But those times had passed, first with his retirement, then with my mother's death, and finally with his move into the retreat house. I suppose most people would have hung on to a great many possessions even then, but my father wasn't one of them.

I set the contents out on my desk. A small brass bell, which had belonged to his grandmother. The pencil sketch of my mother, which he had drawn himself. My mother's wedding ring, and his. The tiny carved stone frog I had played with as a child. Some pencils, and a small pad of sketching paper. Most of the sheets were blank, though there was a half-completed sketch of a sparrow on a window sill. His glasses.

And the magic box.

It had always rested on his desk when I was a boy. I knew what it contained—or at least what it had contained back then. His pocket knife, some more sketching pencils, a kneaded eraser, maybe another sketching pad. Odds and ends that he didn't want cluttering up his desk.

I thought of it as the *magic* box because there was a trick to opening it, a trick he would never divulge. I'd sneaked into his office often when I was nine or ten to examine it, but I'd never learned its secret. It was wooden, and beautifully carved—a bit larger than a Bible. I still didn't know its secret, and I turned it over one way and another, looking for a hint, but found nothing.

In the end I left the frog and the bell and the box on my desk, in the same positions they had stood sentry on his all those years ago. I slid the sketch pad and pencils into a drawer. I didn't know what to do with his glasses. If I kept them, they would just collect dust in a box or drawer somewhere. I should have put them in the church rummage bin, but for some reason I was reluctant to do that.

I put his sketch of my mother on the right corner of my desk, opposite the magic box.

Chapter 10

"Heresy is, fortunately, a matter of opinion in the end. As such it is an indispensable tool for those responsible for maintaining order in the church."

Presbyter Ethan Brine

THERE WERE two things about that conversation with Bee that bothered me.

Even if I decided to put Boyd first, I had no idea how. It didn't necessarily mean I should tell him about the books. It might be better for him if he never found out. And I didn't know enough about the whole situation to decide.

Of course, it was possible that I was just making excuses. I really didn't like the thought of that conversation with him.

"Boyd, I lied to you about that contraband thing. I have some books I shouldn't have."

"And you didn't tell me? Why not?"

"It's complicated."

I just couldn't see that going well.

But there was another, deeper, problem about Bee's approach.

She had completely discounted any question of what I *should* do: of right and wrong. She was only interested in what I wanted.

I was a pastor, for God's sake.

And, besides that, if everybody just did whatever they wanted, chaos would ensue.

I thought of those books in my drawer. *The Great Divorce*, and *The God I Don't Believe In*.

It was way too easy for heresy to infect the mind of the righteous.

I THOUGHT things were as bad as they could get.

I had lied to my friend, held on to illegal books, been threatened with the end of my career by one person, and with "the end of my life as I knew it" by another. I had promised to consider committing a murder. My father had just died. And I was beginning to question my friendship with Bee, just as I was realizing that it might be the best friendship I had.

I couldn't have imagined anything worse.

The Sunday evening service went well. Word had spread, even among the squatters, of my father's death, so I had to accept a barrage of sympathy after the rituals. But it was a fresh sermon, and I hadn't preached in the morning, so I had to pay attention—which was probably a good thing, given my state of mind.

Just as I began, I saw Bee slipping into a seat at the back of the sanctuary. She stayed for the sermon, but left before the blessing ceremony. Apparently she had only come to hear me preach.

After the last of the well-wishers left, I walked home the long way, enjoying a bit of solitude and silence after three hectic days. There was no moon, and the stars dusted the sky in the spaces between the branches overhead. I didn't leave the quiet streets of the village or venture into squatter territory. I just made a circle of the tenant neighborhoods, taking me almost to the village center, then back home.

I came in through the kitchen and was engulfed by the aroma of dinner: fresh-baked loaves on the counter, something simmering on the stove—onions, garlic, tomato. The house was warm after the cool evening air.

Lucky wasn't in the kitchen. I called for him, but he didn't answer, so I decided to go up to my office and change. But I saw him as soon as I entered the living room.

He was sitting on the stairs, about halfway up, motionless. He gave no sign that he knew I had entered the room. There was an expression on his face I hadn't seen before. Something between horror and fear and worry. He was staring at the floor just inside the front doorway.

I took a couple of steps into the room so I could see what he was looking at.

The body was slumped, head and shoulders against the wall, legs spread wide. His left forearm lay at an odd angle on the floor, with the hand palm up. His other arm lay parallel to his body, clutching his walking stick.

His face held the same horror as Lucky's, but multiplied by a thousand or more. A man could have died from such horror alone. But he hadn't. I didn't need to check his pulse, because there was a perfectly circular hole in his chest about six inches across. I could see the bright green of the entryway rug through it.

———

"SO YOU FIRST SAW HIM HERE?"

Dennis was quizzing Lucky at the top of the stairs. Below us, the healers were wrapping up the body to transport it back to the police station. They had been there less than a second before they declared the poor man dead and their chariot changed from the white of an ambulance to the black of a hearse. The hole in his chest had left little doubt.

Lucky had already told us that he'd paused from cooking dinner to go upstairs to use the bathroom. That when he came out he saw the stranger just leaving my office. That the man had fled down the stairs, and that by the time Lucky got to the top of the stairs, the fellow was crumpled where I saw him when I came in, with a hole in his chest. He said he thought he'd heard the kitchen door slam after that, but he had been so horrified by the body that he couldn't be sure.

"So you first saw him here?"

Lucky nodded.

"He was just closing the door behind him."

Dennis' eyebrows bunched together.

"Was he carrying anything?"

"Just his walking stick."

"Are you sure?"

Lucky shrugged.

"Reasonably."

My office door was still ajar. Dennis pulled a handkerchief out of his pocket and used it to push the door open. He motioned for me to go through.

"Tell me if anything's missing."

The room looked much as I had left it. The only difference I could see was that the left bottom drawer in my desk, the one I had stashed the books in, was slightly open. I certainly didn't want to call Dennis' attention to that so I made a show of looking around the room in general.

"I don't think anything's been disturbed."

He handed me his handkerchief.

"Take a look through your cupboards and drawers."

I went over to the cupboard and opened one door after another, peering in. Dennis followed me, and did the same. When I finished, he suggested I look through the desk.

There were six drawers in the desk. One in the center, three down the left side, and two on the right. The bottom one on the right was the largest drawer, the one I had put the books in. I started with the top drawer on the left and searched as slowly and methodically as I could. Dennis stood by, watching me. Lucky wandered over to peruse the open cupboards.

I finished the top drawer on the left and moved to the second one. Dennis examined my father's stone frog.

I moved on to the bottom drawer. Dennis put the frog down and picked up my father's magic box.

"What's in this?"

"I don't know, actually. It was my father's. It used to sit on his desk. He'd keep different odds and ends in it."

"How do you open it?"

"There's some secret trick to it. He would never tell me, and I haven't had time to figure it out."

Dennis turned it over in his hands, looking for a way in.

I moved to the center drawer.

Dennis put the box down.

"You don't have to take all day."

I shrugged and closed the center drawer, then opened the top drawer on the right side.

Dennis picked up the bell.

"This your father's, too?"

"It was his grandmother's."

I couldn't put it off any longer. I closed the top drawer, took a deep breath, and reached for the bottom one.

"What's this?"

It was Lucky. He had found the sliding door at the back of the cabinet. Dennis crossed the room to see it, and I pushed the bottom drawer all the way closed.

I crossed the room to join them, and stood just behind Dennis.

"Nothing missing from the desk," I said.

Dennis was staring at the hidden storage space.

"Did you know this was here? Because we didn't see it when we made the search."

"Actually, I found it *because* of the search. I'd always thought this room was a little short for the building, and your search the other day made me wonder what happened to the extra space. So I experimented with the back of the cupboard and found this."

"And it was bare, like this?"

"From the looks of those shelves I'd say one of the previous pastors collected books."

Dennis nodded to himself.

"And you're sure there was nothing in it?"

DENNIS and his people finally left. The healer's chariot, now a hearse, had gone its way. As soon as it rounded the corner I went in search of Lucky. I found him in the kitchen, scraping burned food from a pot.

He looked up.

"Sorry about dinner. There's some bread and cheese on the table."

"Lucky, can I ask you something?"

He put the pot down.

"What?"

"Just don't get sore at me."

"Okay."

"Is there anything you didn't tell Dennis. I mean . . . I just want to be certain . . . That man, you're sure he wasn't carrying anything when he left my office?"

"I'm sure."

"And you have no idea who he is?"

He looked at me thoughtfully.

"None."

I grabbed a piece of cheese and wandered into the living room, over to the rug at the bottom of the stairs. There was no sign that the body had ever been there. No blood at all, in spite of the enormous hole in the man's chest. For some reason that gave me an odd sense of déjà vu.

I took the steps two at a time to my office. I closed the door behind me and went directly to my desk. I pulled the left side bottom drawer open.

It was completely empty.

Chapter 11

"A society which grants all power to a few must at least appear to balance that power. The short domination officially divided the various sources of power—ownership, use of violence, knowledge, education, control of communications—between the holders, the government, and the church. There were unofficial powers as well: sorcerers' guilds, clandestine religions, the Humans, the Order of Jerubbaal, and others—including, of course, the most important one of all."

Dorothy Kenning, *The Short Domination: A Student Primer*

"So most of this stuff was your dad's?"

Bee was surveying the surface of my desk. She had come by to convince me to visit Anna with her again. I took her up to my office and told her about the body.

It turned out there was very little to tell. I didn't know who the victim was, why he had come into my house, where the books had gone, who had killed him, or why. So our conversation had dwindled.

"Most of it," I said.

"That's a very nice walking stick."

"He had it custom made before I was born. It's a bit out of style now."

"But classy, in an understated way. Will you start carrying it?"

"I'm not really into the fads of fashion."

She shrugged.

"I think it fits you perfectly."

She picked up the picture of my mother.

"I'd forgotten what a good artist he was."

"He had a lot of practice. He hardly went anywhere without his sketchpad."

"He certainly caught her essence. Your mother was a beautiful woman."

She pulled the sketch closer to her face and squinted at it.

"Say, you remember how your dad kept saying that your mom would tell you something?"

"He was hallucinating toward the end."

"What if he wasn't?"

"He was."

"What if he was being sneaky? What if he was trying to tell you something?"

I was interested in spite of myself.

"What do you mean?"

"Under his signature here, in the corner where artists usually put the date. It's not a date. It looks like some kind of code."

I laughed.

"Something like 'H-E-Z-3-colon-1-8'?"

She slumped.

"Yes, exactly like that. What does it mean?"

"It's kind of a joke, and kind of a pun, I guess. The joke part is that it's a scripture reference. Like Matthias 3:18."

"Joshua wept?"

"Right. Only most people just hear those references spoken, in a sermon or something, but in seminary, where we constantly reference Bible verses for study purposes, we use the written notation."

"So your dad went to seminary?"

"When he was young, before he met my mother and they decided to work for the Franklyns. He never completed his degree."

"And this verse. What does it say?"

"That's the joke. The 'Hez' stands for Hezekiah, so the reference is to Hezekiah 3:18, but there *is* no book of Hezekiah in the Bible."

"Hilarious so far."

"It was a private joke between my father and my mother. If he expressed an opinion that she thought was unfounded, she would say he got it from Hezekiah 3:18, which was a way of saying it was just my dad's unsupported opinion. Or sometimes she'd say 'the gospel according to Jeffrey'. Sometimes he would beat her to the punch, and quote the same verse as evidence— meaning 'according to me'."

"And the 'pun' part?"

"The drawing is a sketch of my mother, a sketch *he* drew. It's my mother 'according to Jeffrey'."

She nodded thoughtfully, and put the sketch back on my desk.

"They had a good marriage, didn't they?"

"They did."

I took a breath.

"Would you be offended if I asked you something a little personal?"

She stiffened a little.

"I guess we're going to find out."

"Were you . . . I mean, you were . . . were *chosen*, right?"

She relaxed.

"I can read and write and even do some 'rithmatic."

"Sorry for asking. I just realized I never knew."

"And you thought you'd better check before hanging out with me anymore?"

I felt myself blush.

I HADN'T GUESSED Bee's reasons for that visit to Anna.

A Lazarus Stone can be deceptive. It keeps you alive. It even makes you look fairly healthy. If I hadn't known Anna as well as I did, I might have been fooled. But she was clearly in pain, a lot of pain. Beyond that, she was miserable emotionally—partly because she felt she was being forced to live past her time. But there was something else, something she wouldn't tell us.

I gathered she felt she was being used in some way, that she was being forced to live on for some purpose that she didn't endorse. But that was as much as we could get out of her.

Bee's purposes, on the other hand, became absolutely clear.

We had chatted with Anna for about twenty minutes, almost as long as her healer would allow. She'd had tea served, and we had rehearsed old memories of our time as children on the estate. We'd even laughed a little, which I saw as a good sign for Anna.

I was sitting on the right side of her bed. Bee had pulled a chair around to the left side, and held Anna's hand through most of our visit.

I thought Anna looked like she was tiring, and motioned to Bee that we should go.

Bee nodded, and suddenly looked very worried.

Facial expressions can be very compelling. You tend to focus on them, and if you don't understand them you can find yourself completely absorbed in the question of what they mean. I was so busy trying to figure out why that expression was on Bee's face that I didn't see her hand pick up the stone and move it toward her bag.

Anna's healer burst into the room.

"Please don't move the Lazarus Stone!"

Bee looked down at the stone, with apparent surprise.

"Oh! Sorry."

She placed it back where it had been.

The healer came around the bed, and adjusted the stone's position.

"It would be best if you didn't touch it at all," he said.

Bee smiled up at him.

"Of course. I . . . I didn't realize."

BEE WAS unrepentant on the trip back to town.

"Well, I guess that's that. We won't be able to steal the stone, unless we find a way to drug the healers while we do it."

"Don't be ridiculous."

"I wasn't serious. But now we have to find another way. Maybe there are strings we can pull."

"I thought it was 'none of your business'."

"It's none of my business what you do or don't do as her pastor. It's definitely my business what I do as her friend."

I didn't respond. We rode in silence until we were almost at the edge of the village. I stopped the chariot.

Bee stepped down to the street, then looked up at me.

"Dinner tonight, at my place, after your services?"

"I'm not sure that would look right."

She put her hand on my arm.

"I've hired a local cook, a tenant. He'll be there the whole time. So you won't have to worry about gossip."

I hesitated. The truth was, I had something I'd been meaning to ask her.

"Can we agree to talk about something other than Anna?"

"So where do you know Will Terren from?"

I was standing in front of Chief Tho's desk again, and he was leaning back with his hands behind his head. On my way through town, I had been stopped by the same policeman who had blocked my door while Dennis searched my house, and he had brought me to the station.

"Will Terren?"

The chief nodded.

"Will Terren. The fellow found dead in your house. Though that's not his real name, as you probably know."

"I don't know any Will Terren."

"Well, that's the name in his wallet. He wears the logo of the Gate Corporation. They're located back east. So we checked with them. They don't know any Will Terren. That logo on his forehead's way too nice for a squatter, and if he was a tenant, they'd know him. So he must be someone else."

He paused, and squinted at me.

"Considering our special relationship, I thought maybe you could help me with that."

"The first time I saw him, Chief, he had a hole in his chest."

He sat up then and folded those big hands in front of him on the desk.

"You expect me to believe that a man is murdered in your house and you have no idea who he is?"

"None."

"And you have no idea how he was killed . . ."

"Not a clue."

" . . .or who killed him . . ."

"Nope."

" . . .or why he was there?"

"Not an inkling."

He looked me over.

"I think we both know *why* he was there, at least. He was looking for something—something you have that I want."

"I don't have any books, Chief."

He chuckled.

"Well, that's interesting. Because I don't recall ever mentioning books."

Damn.

I forced myself to meet his gaze and put a puzzled expression on my face.

"Dennis didn't tell you about the hiding place in my office?"

The look of triumph left his face.

"Why don't you just refresh my memory."

"We found this hiding place, a sliding panel at the back of a cupboard. There were shelves in it, the right size to store books. Apparently one of my predecessors was a collector."

"And you didn't know this hiding place was there?"

"Not until after Dennis searched my house."

I decided to press my advantage.

"So this stuff you think I've got. It *is* books?"

He gave me a long, thoughtful stare.

"You know full well it is. I don't fool that easily, son. I'll check with Detective Troy. But even if you showed him this 'secret space'—and even if it's filled with empty shelves meant for books—that doesn't mean you don't have the books I'm looking for. And I'm beginning to think you may have a foolish idea in your head. If you're thinking you're safe as long as you've got those books and I still need them, your focus is a bit narrow."

"I don't understand."

"There are plenty of ways I can hurt you indirectly. That young lady you've been spending so much time with, for example. Or how about that servant of yours, the last person to see your murdered guest alive?"

And at that moment I did something entirely by instinct that I'm ashamed of to this day. It may have been my sense of who was more vulnerable. It may have just been misplaced chivalry. It may have been something else. But the words were out of my mouth before I thought.

"Leave Lucky out of this!"

And he reacted just the way I wanted him to.

"So," he said. "Lucky." Then he grinned and drew a finger across his neck. "Well, my young friend, if you're so concerned about Lucky, you know what you have to do."

Chapter 12

I WAS WORRIED that the question I had for Bee could be taken the wrong way, so I found myself a bit off-stride from the moment she greeted me at the door.

She had done something different with her hair. I couldn't decide what it was, but it was very nice. When I'd first seen her at the Humble Monk, she had been far too put-together for me to form any opinion of her looks. And since then she had just been my childhood pal. But now I could see that she was actually quite attractive.

And that just made my question harder to ask. In fact, I wasn't entirely sure that I *would* ask it.

The house she had rented was roomier and lighter than the parsonage, and better maintained. The wood floors were highly polished, the brightly colored rugs had no sign of frayed fringes, and I was fairly certain that at least two of the famous paintings on the walls were originals.

She took me into the dining room, and lit the candles on the table.

"I thought we'd have some real flames. My status in the holder world probably wouldn't allow me a real fireplace, and this house doesn't have one anyway. But I can manage a couple of candles at dinner occasionally."

For a moment I thought she might be pulling rank on me, but then she gave me a conspiratorial grin, and I knew better. Besides, as minor clergy I ranked somewhere between tenant and holder, and could probably have gotten away with a candle or two myself, if I cared to.

The cook she had hired was better than Lucky, though.

Our conversation ranged from childhood memories to recent events. She told me some stories about her mother, and I reciprocated with tales of my parents. We shared some affectionate but less than flattering memories of Boyd as a kid.

I told her about my conversation with Chief Tho, and we speculated about the murder. She was true to her word, and never mentioned Anna, or her request. But she did want to talk about my father's request.

"The thing is," she said, "I *did* promise him, so I feel obligated to at least take the trouble to see if there's anything to it."

"But you don't even know what it was you promised."

"Not for sure. But it was pretty clear that he was afraid you would do something before you heard from your mother."

"Who is dead. I was there. I know."

"Right. So maybe that part was just in his head. But what about the other part? What was it he didn't want you to do?"

"I don't know. I suppose he wanted me to find something, maybe."

"Those books?"

"I don't see how. They were left by some previous pastor, almost certainly. And I can't imagine how he would have known they were there, let alone how he would connect them to my mother."

"So something else. Have you opened that 'magic box' yet?"

"I haven't had the time. I'm not going to break into it. It's too beautiful, and I'm fond of the memories."

"I think you should take the time. What if I come over tomorrow afternoon and help?"

I put up my hands.

"Okay. I surrender. Tomorrow afternoon. On the condition that we change the subject now."

"It's a deal. So what do you want to talk about instead?"

That was my moment.

"Okay. This is a bit silly, but I hate not being clear about the facts . . ."

"I hadn't noticed."

"And when we were visiting my father, you called my mother 'Aunt Mary,' and then I remembered that when we were kids I called your mother 'Aunt Joan,' and it occurred to me that maybe I hadn't realized that—"

"We're not."

"So, to be clear . . ."

"We're not cousins. We're not blood relations of any kind. Your mother and my mother were best friends their whole lives. They were as close as sisters. But 'Aunt' was just a kind of honorary title."

I nodded.

"I see."

I NEARLY FORGOT my lunch date with Dennis the next day.

By the time I got to the Humble Monk, he was already seated. He looked up from his menu.

"I almost ordered without you."

"Yeah. Sorry. With all that's happened it's amazing I remembered at all."

He considered that.

"You *have* been through a lot lately. How are you holding up?"

"Just barely. The funeral's tomorrow, and there doesn't seem to be a lot I can do about most of the other stuff. Still . . ."

"Right."

The waitress appeared and took our orders. Dennis opted for the turkey Reuben; I had the roast chicken.

When she left, I asked Dennis about the investigation. He shrugged.

"It's all over the place. The victim had a name on him, but as near as we can tell there's no such person. He was apparently a regular at the Thirsty Angel—that place at the edge of squatter land—so we're going to question the other regulars and the staff there."

"What made that hole in his chest?"

"We haven't a clue. Something like a police rod, possibly, but no police rod is that powerful. There are always rumors of sorcerers among the squatters who can produce custom rods, but I've been around a long time and I've yet to see one."

"A sorcerer, or a custom rod?"

"Either. And other than that . . . You want to come in tomorrow morning, look at the body again? Give me a fresh set of eyes?"

"If you think it might help. I'd sure like to know why he was in my house."

"Probably the same reason the burglar was, even if they aren't the same person."

"So he didn't find what he was looking for the first time around, came back, and this time someone followed him?"

"Or the person who killed him was the original burglar."

"But why did they kill him? Lucky said he wasn't carrying anything."

"Maybe there was another reason. Or maybe it was small enough to put in a pocket. So he got past Lucky with it, but whoever killed him . . ."

I decided to risk it.

"Chief Tho thinks I have *books*. But you couldn't put books in your pocket."

Dennis was suddenly very interested.

"How well did you search that secret storage space before the murder?"

"I looked it over. I wouldn't say 'searched' really. I suppose I could have missed something, if it was small."

He contemplated that while he chewed and swallowed.

"It's a possibility. But it doesn't help at the moment. Do me a favor, though. Give it a good search, and let me know if you find anything."

"But if the guy took it . . ."

"He might not have found it. It might still be there."

"Okay. I'll look."

He relaxed and shot me a wicked grin.

"So how are you getting along with your new girlfriend?"

———

As a child, I had been fascinated by the abstract designs carved into my father's magic box.

The sides were carved with groups of vertical ridges of varying width from top to bottom. In the spaces between these groups there were oblong shapes of varying size, mostly ovals, with one or two more complex decorations interspersed. The top of the box had several rounded heart-shapes in the center, surrounded by a variety of short thin triangles radiating outward. Partial ovals, similar to the ones on the sides, extended from the heart-shapes at various angles.

That description probably sounds uninspired, but the composition was masterful, and the effect was lovely. I remember being mesmerized by the design as a boy—between my attempts to push at the heart-shapes and ridges in hopes of discovering the secret latch.

I'd brought the box down to the living room so Bee and I could investigate it over tea and some of Lucky's cookies. We were taking turns prodding, turning, shaking, and examining it, without making any progress.

"So, about Anna . . ."

"I thought we agreed not to talk about that."

"We agreed not to talk about it during dinner last night. Not forever."

"There's really nothing we can do. And probably nothing we should do."

"I don't believe that."

Bee had turned the box upside down, and was carefully examining the bottom.

"So when your father opened this, can you remember how he held it?"

"Yes. It was exactly the same every time I saw him do it."

Her eyes brightened.

"Really? Can you show me?"

I took the box, stood up, held it behind my back for a moment, then swung it around in front of me.

"Ta-da!"

She scowled.

"So not much help."

"Unfortunately."

"Anna's in pain," Bee said. "And she's miserable. And if someone hadn't decided—without consulting her—to intervene, she would have died of natural causes."

"We can't change that."

"It's not right."

"It's a miracle. How can it be wrong?"

"A common miracle. The person who decided could have been wrong."

So Bee knew about common miracles as well. There was hardly any advantage to being in the clergy any more.

"Funny," I replied, "that's what Anna said. But it doesn't matter. You saw what happened when you tried to interfere yesterday."

"We just have to figure out a different approach, that's all."

I thumped the box down on the table in frustration.

"I give up."

"On what," Lucky asked, "exactly?" He was standing behind me with a fresh pot of tea.

I gestured toward the box.

"Dad's box. We can't figure out its secret."

A hint of amusement crossed his face.

"It was only ever a secret from you, Lad. He never told you, even after you were grown?"

"You know how to open it?"

"Of course. I was his chief assistant."

"Are you going to tell us, or just stand there gloating?"

"I'll be right back."

He went upstairs and returned almost immediately, carrying the stone frog from my desk.

He placed it on one of the heart shapes, which perfectly fit the lily-pad at the base of the statue.

And suddenly the carvings were transformed.

It was nothing miraculous—or perhaps it was, but the miracle was in my mind.

What I had always seen as a meaningless but beautiful collection of shapes and lines, I suddenly saw as an abstract depiction of a pond. The heart shapes were lily pads. The ovals were fish. The ridges and triangles were reeds. There was even an abstract frog in the water.

We heard a faint click, and Lucky lifted the top of the box.

Chapter 13

"Kinde's compulsive curiosity could lead him to see what others might miss but it could also cause him to waste time and energy looking for what wasn't there."

Silas Redford, *The Real Adam Kinde: An Experiment in Biography*

EARLIER THAT AFTERNOON, before Bee arrived, I had kept my promise to Dennis to search the secret space in my office. It seemed pointless to me. Whoever killed that man also had the books now, and they were almost certainly what he had come for.

But I'd promised.

I slid the panel open, and worked my way along every shelf, by sight and feel, for anything we might have missed earlier.

It wasn't a comfortable search. The opening was about four feet wide, but the space itself was ten feet wide—which meant that it extended two feet past the opening to the right, and four feet past the opening to the left.

Since the space in front of the shelves was only a little more than a foot deep, it was difficult to see or reach all the way to the end of that four feet. Not impossible, but it involved getting into difficult positions.

My first search turned up nothing, and I almost left it at that, but then it occurred to me that something might be fastened to the underside of a shelf, so I went over the whole space again, this time mostly by touch.

Then I wondered if something might be attached to the front wall. That presented a problem, since most of the front wall was covered by the sliding panel.

I couldn't get the panel loose, so in the end I managed to squeeze into the space, facing out, and slid the panel almost closed so I could feel the wall behind it. Even then I couldn't reach all the way to the floor.

But by then I no longer cared.

I decided that would have to do, and if Dennis wanted anything more thorough, he could do it himself.

<hr>

LUCKY PUT the open box down on the coffee table, and we went through the contents.

On top were several sketches, one rather good one of my father's healer. I made a mental note to send it to him. The others were still-lifes: a bottle next to an apple, the stone frog in its place on the magic box, his Bible and pocketknife next to the sketch of my mother.

That last one was impressive because the sketch of my mother was at a forty-five degree angle, so he had produced a sketch of a sketch, but distorted by perspective.

His Bible was under the sketches, and took up most of the space in the box. Bee had the same first thought I did about that.

"Why did he put his Bible in there?"

It was a good question. If he had simply left it out, it would have been turned in automatically by the retreat center. Everyone's Bible was turned in at death. It didn't make much difference in this case, since the center would have turned it in to the local church—which was mine—to be reissued. Still, it was a bit odd of him to hide it away like that.

But then I remembered my talk with him the previous Thursday.

"He was getting paranoid toward the end. The last time I saw him, before you and I visited, he took my Bible away from me and stuck it in a drawer. Then he whispered to me, as though he thought we could be overheard. I didn't make much of it at the time, but now I think he believed our Bibles were listening to us."

"So he locked it in the box, to keep it from listening?"

Lucky nodded.

"He told me so," he said, "the last time I visited him. He thought someone was listening, and thought it might be through my Bible, so he put it in a drawer."

Next to the Bible were his pocketknife and a few odds and ends: sketching pencils, the kneaded eraser I remembered, a pair of cuff-links, a polished stone my mother had given him.

Bee sighed.

"Well, I guess that's it."

"Yeah," I said. "You're off the hook."

I MET Dennis the next morning at the police station.

He took me in the opposite direction from his office,

through a long corridor that ended in a stairway leading down to the dank basement and a large room with a stone floor.

"The healer's finished with him, but I asked him to wait until I could look him over for myself."

The body was laid out on a metal table in the middle of the room. There was a strong scent of antiseptic in the air. The healer stood silently to one side. Dennis pulled the blanket down to the victim's waist, revealing the hole in his bare chest.

"No real question about the cause of death," he said.

"I suppose not."

"You don't recognize him, I suppose?"

"I can't say I do."

"He's pretty clearly not a squatter, so that might mean something in itself. Wouldn't you remember if he had attended Sunday morning services?"

"Interesting. I'm pretty sure I would, if for no other reason than the walking stick."

"The walking stick?"

"He looks too young to need one. So it's an affectation."

"I'd say stylish."

"I'm just saying I think I'd have noticed."

The furrow between Dennis' eyes deepened.

"You ought to try carrying one. It might impress your girl."

I changed the subject.

"So if he didn't come to my services, that means he was getting his Bible blessed elsewhere."

"It's something."

Dennis scratched his neck and stared at the body.

"I looked him over at the parsonage, before they took him away. I didn't see anything useful then. I can't say I expect to see anything now. That's why I brought you along. Take your time, and don't be afraid to speak up or ask questions. You never know what I might be missing."

I walked around the body, viewing it from various angles.

He was fairly young—about my age, really. And he had been in fairly good shape. His hair was blond, cut in the latest ragged fashion among tenants and sometimes even holders. He sported a tiny mustache—so thin and light in color that it was almost invisible.

His eyebrows were also thin and light, in contrast to the dark logo above the right one. There were beads of condensation on his forehead.

I leaned closer and squinted at the logo.

"Whose logo did you say this was?"

"The Gate Corporation. Back East."

It depicted two posts with a gate, such as one might see in a garden fence, swung half open between them. The gate itself was in the form of a capital G.

Something about the right post bothered me.

I bent closer.

"Dennis, would it be okay if I ... Could I have a damp cloth, and maybe some soap?"

Dennis shot a glance at the healer, who shrugged and gestured to a basin at the side of the room.

Dennis handed me a cloth, and I wiped the condensation away from the victim's forehead. The edge of the post was a bit blurred.

"Yes. I think ..."

I scrubbed at the corner of the logo, and with a little effort, it began to come off.

Dennis' mouth dropped open.

"A fake logo? No wonder we couldn't trace him."

I remembered my first impression of Bee, in the Humble Monk, and it gave me an idea.

"Let's check his hands."

But there was no logo on either hand, no Miracle Skin or makeup covering a logo. We turned our attention back to his forehead, and scrubbed above each eyebrow thoroughly. Nothing.

Chapter 14

"The real struggle comes when we are faced with competing virtues. Should I seek justice over the care of others? Should I protect a career that positions me to help countless others, or protect a friend? We tend to think this kind of choice is rare, but it is a kind we face daily."

Adam Kinde, *The Collected Sermons of Adam Kinde*

"I CAN ONLY THINK of two possibilities . . ."

We were back upstairs, in Dennis' office. He had stopped by the staff room and poured out two cups of coffee on the way. He pushed one across the desk at me.

". . . two possibilities," he said, "one of which seems very unlikely. But the other strains credulity."

I took a sip. He had been right the other day. The coffee was nasty.

"So the unlikely one is . . .?"

"He's a holder. He doesn't have a logo because he doesn't need one, and, like most holders, he flaunts the fact."

"Why is that unlikely?"

"Two reasons. First, he apparently *does* need one, since no one has recognized him."

"Maybe he's just from far enough away—"

He held up his hand.

"And second, why would a holder be wearing a fake logo showing his allegiance to *another* holder?"

"As a disguise. Whatever he was doing in the parsonage, it was clearly something he didn't want to be known."

He considered that.

"Maybe. I like it better than the other possibility."

"And that is . . .?"

"Don't laugh."

"Okay."

"He might just be a Human."

I almost did laugh.

"He's obviously a human."

"I mean a Human with a capital H."

"Sorry," I said. "You lost me."

"Actually, that makes it easier to explain—you won't have a bunch of weird ideas to correct."

He took a long sip of whatever it was in our coffee mugs.

"There's this rumor, or myth, or tall tale—take your pick— that this group of people exists. People who call themselves simply 'Humans'."

"With a capital H."

"Exactly. They're supposedly infidels, but not like the half-crazed type you find out in the wild, or the bizarre cults you sometimes get in squatter territory. They're supposed to be quite civilized, except for their strange beliefs and their absolute refusal to wear a logo."

I gave up on my coffee and put it down.

"Where would people like that possibly live?"

"That's the standard question, whenever this rumor surfaces. It's clearly impossible. The only place you can live a civilized life is among tenants or holders. And to do that, you have to wear a logo."

"Or a fake one."

"Except that it doesn't make sense to wear a fake one. If you belong to a group which absolutely refuses to wear a logo, presumably on principle, then it would be very strange to live your life *always* wearing a fake one."

"Unless you only put on the fake one when you have to visit tenant territory."

"Which brings us full circle. Where do you live a civilized life the rest of the time?"

He stared morosely at his mug before continuing.

"So," he said, "he's either a disguised holder or a disguised Human, I guess. Has Lucky said anything more about what happened?"

"That's an abrupt change of subject."

"It's just—his story is a bit hard to believe the way he told it."

"Really?"

"He swore the victim wasn't carrying anything when he came out of your office—"

"Wasn't carrying anything *in his hands*."

"Right. So unless it was something very small, which we have no evidence of, there seems to be no reason for the guy to be there."

"That's it?"

"Also, he says he didn't see the killing. But he was only a few feet from the top of the stairs, and he had every reason to hurry after the guy. So why didn't he reach the top of the stairs before whatever killed the guy . . . *killed* the guy?"

"It was fortunate running, ahhh, running into you like this, Pastor Kinde."

We were seated facing each other in Presbyter Brines' chariot, high above the Pacific Coast. The sky above us was gray, as was the ocean below. As the presbyter spoke, a pelican plummeted into the waves after a fish.

His guardian angel had pulled the chariot up in front of the police station just as I was leaving and gestured for me to get into the back. Brine had nodded at me without saying a word and the chariot had taken to the air, heading southwest over the Valley and the mountains to the sea.

I'd decided it must be up to me to start the conversation.

"Your angel can drive a chariot?"

He'd given me an uninterested glance.

"Not the same as you or I . . . can't move physical objects directly, of course. They learn, ahhh, learn whatever skills their duties require. You don't think cherubim were originally created to harvest wheat?"

I'd started to speak again, but he had silenced me with a wave of his hand. So we'd traveled on in silence.

But apparently he was now ready to talk. His eyes moved from the view below us and fixed on me.

"There have been some, ahhh, some developments recently that I would like to discuss with you."

"Developments?"

"Yes." He blinked at me. "Developments."

I waited for him to speak again, but his attention appeared to be drifting.

"What kind of developments?"

"Developments of a . . . of, shall we say, of an *organizational* nature."

"Within the church, you mean?"

"Ahhh. Very good. Very good. So you understand?"

"It might be helpful," I said, "if you could fill in the details."

"The details. Yes . . ." His eyes wandered to the waves crashing on the beach below. "We—the church council, that is —we're doing some *restructuring* locally . . ."

"Restructuring."

"Restructuring. We're adding a new ministry, a position supervising all of the churches in the San Fernando Valley."

"And this new person is going to be supervising me."

His eyes jerked back to me. He seemed a bit startled.

"Oh, no, my good, ahhh, good man. Not at all."

"I don't understand."

"We have a really fine, an excellent crop of seminary students coming up. Very talented."

"And?"

"We need positions for them . . . for them to start out in. Positions like the one you are currently in."

"I'm being fired?"

"I don't want to take too much credit, of course, but it was my suggestion, my suggestion that you be, ahhh, be made the new supervisor."

I was stumped.

"You're offering me a *promotion*?"

"We need your current position for a new man, you see . . ."

"But after our last conversation I thought . . ."

"Ahhh, well. That would be a consideration, of course. Were you to prove uncooperative on that matter I might be forced . . . forced to reconsider my suggestion."

"And if I don't want the promotion?"

"Well, as I said, we do have plans . . . *other* plans . . . for your current position."

He reached over and patted my knee.

"I'll give you a . . . shall we say, a day? Yes. A day to—to think it over. We'll meet for lunch. Tomorrow. At the Humble Monk.

You can bring them along then. Wrapped up, of course . . . no need to call attention."

He returned his gaze to the sea below.

———

DENNIS WAS WAITING by my chariot when Brine's angel brought me back. He didn't look happy.

I asked him what was wrong and he scowled.

"We need to talk."

He led me back into his office again, and motioned me to sit.

"You know what I said earlier, about Lucky's story?"

"Yes?"

"I need you to keep that conversation confidential. Especially from Lucky."

"Really? Why?"

"I had one of my men question the proprietor of the Thirsty Angel."

"And?"

"And Lucky's name came up. Apparently he's something of a regular there, as well."

"That doesn't necessarily mean—"

"I'm not through. He apparently spent a lot of time talking to our victim there over the last few weeks."

I thought about that. Lucky wasn't the type to lie, let alone commit murder.

"There must be some mistake."

"I figured you'd say that. I don't blame you. But it looks pretty solid. Not like, 'Oh, he looked a little like' or 'I thought maybe'. He called Lucky by name, said he was a regular, gave a perfect description of our victim, and showed my man the table where they drank together."

"I still don't believe it."

"Your privilege. I don't want to believe it either. But I do have to ask you to keep your mouth shut around Lucky. I'm going to do everything I can to get to the bottom of this before we have to act, but if the chief hears about it, and it turns out you tipped Lucky off, it won't be good for Lucky—or for either of us."

He ran a hand through his hair.

"The good news is that there've been several murders among the squatters in the last year or so that might be related."

"And that's good news because . . ."

"Because it really doesn't sound like Lucky. They were all killed with something like a police rod."

"Only more powerful?"

"It looks like. Nothing as extreme as our victim so far, but lethal. So it's possible, even likely, there's a connection."

"I really don't like keeping things from Lucky, Dennis."

He shrugged.

Chapter 15

"Privacy was another right which varied by status. Squatters could have readings used against them without their permission but had no right to demand one for their defense. Holders, judges, police, and members of the clergy could demand a reading or refuse one. Their servants and tenants could usually refuse a reading, but had no clear right to request it."

Dorothy Kenning, *The Short Domination: A Student Primer*

My lunch with Bee was not a comfort.

My father's funeral was scheduled for one thirty, so we met early, at the park across the street from the church. Lucky had provided egg salad sandwiches, lemonade, and carrot cake. We sat on the grass, under the largest and oldest tree. The day was warmer than usual for the time of year, so the light breeze didn't bother us.

Bee was beginning to be a problem for me. I was very fond of her, and I found it impossible to believe that she wasn't a good person, which made things difficult when she constantly pushed views that bordered on heresy. My role as a pastor required me to be above reproach in theological matters. But I was beginning to find some of her arguments compelling—all too compelling.

I told her about my conversation with Dennis concerning Lucky.

She held a hand up while she chewed and swallowed a mouthful of sandwich before speaking.

"Lucky? Impossible."

"That's what I said. And Dennis wants to agree. But so far it doesn't look good."

"What does Lucky say about all this?"

"Dennis asked me not to tell him until they could finish investigating."

"That's hardly fair."

"It's complicated. If he's completely innocent, Dennis will prove it."

"You're not saying he might be guilty?"

"He *is* human, after all."

"What does that mean? This isn't about the sermon you preached Sunday night?"

"I wasn't thinking about that, but yes, I guess it's related."

"So Lucky's evil, just because he's human?"

"Well, he's definitely a sinner, like anyone else."

"And that makes him capable of murder?"

"I'm not saying he did it. I'm just saying it's not impossible."

"So what about me? You think *I'm* capable of murder?"

"I'm just telling you what the scriptures say."

"'All have sinned, and come short of the glory of God?'"

"I didn't make that up."

"But did you ever ask yourself what it *means*?"

"I think it's pretty clear."

"Really? What exactly is a 'sin'?"

"Seriously? You don't know?"

"You're the theologian. Humor me."

"Oh. Well, the Greek word for sin means 'to miss the mark,' like in archery."

"And what, exactly, is this 'mark,' this bullseye?"

"It's right there in the verse: 'the glory of God'."

"So to sin is to fall short of the 'glory of God'?"

"Yes."

"And the 'glory of God' is the standard?"

"Yes."

"And would the 'glory of God' be a pretty high standard?"

"Incredibly high."

"Less than perfect?"

I considered.

"Well, no. God's glory, as a moral standard, would have to be absolute perfection."

"So what that verse says is 'nobody's perfect'."

"I suppose you could put it that way, but—"

She leaned forward.

"So how do you get from 'nobody's perfect' to 'everyone's a potential murderer'?"

THE FUNERAL WAS A SIMPLE, short affair. Only a few people attended. Aside from myself and Bee and Boyd, there was Dennis, who came to support me—he never knew my father.

Dad's healer was there, and just one other member of the congregation—a small, elderly man with thinning hair and wire-rimmed glasses. I couldn't have told you his name, but I could tell you the exact seat he habitually sat in, that he always listened intently to the sermon, and that he sang the hymns with gusto.

He approached me after the service and shook my hand.

"Your father was a fine man, pastor. It was a privilege to know him. My condolences."

"Thank you. Did you know him well?"

"We had a business relationship. My shop is in the village. So, no. Not *well*, but he made a great impression on me."

Later that afternoon I sat at my desk, staring blankly at the tree branch just outside my window while I pondered the growing problem that was Bee.

A wasp buzzed against the glass. It had somehow gotten into the house and upstairs into my inner sanctum.

Bee was quite probably a heretic, but that wasn't what bothered me. Half the tenants and holders I knew were heretics to some extent. I suspected that heresies of one kind or another lurked in the minds of most clergy.

No. It wasn't that.

I watched the wasp for a time, then got up and opened the window to let it out.

So what was it? Her impulsiveness? The way she tried to grab the Lazarus Stone?

No. Or, rather, not *simply* that, or the heresy, or the way she took over the night my father died. It was the whole picture— and it was something else, as well.

I was a pastor, after all. I had to keep up appearances, be careful about the company I kept. That was half of it.

The other half was that I didn't really want to, not in this case. She was a childhood friend, after all. She was . . . she was *Bee*.

The front door crashed open, and rapid footsteps thundered up the stairs.

I was out of my chair and at the door in a second, but not

before Chief Tho and two of his officers were past me and halfway to Lucky's room.

When I got to his doorway they were already turning the place upside down. One officer was pulling drawers out of Lucky's dresser and dumping the contents out on the floor. The other one tipped the bed up on edge and searched the underside. The chief was rummaging through the closet.

"Hey!" I said. "What's going on?"

They didn't respond, or even pause in their search. It was as if I wasn't there.

It was the chief who finally spoke.

"And here we have it!"

He turned, grinning, and held up a police rod. At first I didn't understand, and then I saw that his own rod was still hanging from his belt.

"Where's your lucky friend, Pastor?"

He didn't wait for an answer but pushed past me, and almost ran into Lucky coming up the hallway. He recovered himself and grabbed Lucky's arm.

Lucky surveyed the hallway with a panicked gaze which finally came to rest on my hands, and then unaccountably relaxed a bit. He seemed to be trying to remember something.

The chief pulled out a pair of handcuffs.

"Das Baethan, I'm arresting you on suspicion of the murder of Will Terren."

Lucky nodded, but he still seemed preoccupied, and tense about whatever was on his mind.

"You don't need those, Chief. I'll cooperate."

The chief hesitated, then shrugged and put the cuffs away.

The tension went out of Lucky like a sigh. He turned and walked quietly down the stairs to the waiting police chariot.

I was left on the front steps with the feeling that I had just missed something important.

THE OFFICER on the front desk knew me, and knew I was Dennis' friend. He looked up and waved me through.

"In his office."

I nodded my thanks without slowing down.

I was halfway there when the chief called after me.

"Pastor!"

I stopped and turned around. He was standing in his doorway.

"Detective Troy is busy at the moment. Perhaps I can help."

He motioned me to come back.

I followed him into his office. He leaned back in his chair and swung those boots up on the desk, next to the rod he'd held up in Lucky's room.

He pointed at the rod.

"This doesn't look good for your friend."

I met his gaze.

"I don't believe that's Lucky's."

"You were there when I found it."

"I was there when you *claimed* to find it."

He chuckled.

"It's not a real police rod, you know. It looks pretty close, but the weight's wrong, and I'm willing to bet it's a *lot* deadlier."

"You mean it's not iron?"

"Police rods aren't iron, either—though they're made to look like it."

"And you're willing to bet it's deadlier?"

"That's what I said."

"So you haven't tested it yet."

He chuckled again. A self-satisfied little chuckle, with his chin on his chest.

"Here's the deal. Your friend claims not to have seen the murder, yet he was clearly close enough to do just that. He claims the victim came out of your office empty-handed, yet I'm quite sure that he was killed for something he found there. And on top of all that, it turns out he has the murder weapon in his closet."

He swung his feet off the desk and leaned toward me.

"Now, Pastor, do you want to help your friend or not?"

"Of course I want to help him. But if this is still about those books, I can't. I've already told you the truth. I don't have them, and I wouldn't know where to start looking for them. Dennis has searched the house, I've searched the house—and even found an old hiding place for books. But there's nothing in it."

He shook his head at me.

"The case is pretty tight, and the hearing's tomorrow afternoon. Unless I find a real good reason to intervene before then, the execution will be immediately after. I'd advise you to start thinking more creatively."

So I did.

"You're forgetting that I'm ordained, and that Lucky is a member of my household. I can demand that he be allowed to consult the Book of Deeds."

I expected that to deflate him, but he just smiled.

"You may be an expert in theology, Pastor, but you don't know much about the law."

ONCE I ESCAPED Chief Tho's presence I made a beeline for Dennis. But he wasn't in his office, and no one seemed to know where he had gone.

I asked the desk sergeant when I could see Lucky.

He gave me his sympathetic look.

"Not right away, for sure. Just between us, I wouldn't count on it."

"But surely . . ."

"There's a 'no visitors' order in place, and the chief hasn't said for how long."

"I get that. For friends, for relatives if he had any—even for his employer. But I'm also his *pastor*. Surely he can have spiritual counseling?"

He just shrugged.

I turned to leave, then remembered what I had brought with me. I put Lucky's Bible on the counter.

"Could you at least give him this?"

He picked it up.

"I'll check with the chief."

I wandered out the door, trying to think what else I could do, and stopped just outside, staring at the sky. I could smell the pines on the other side of the square. Somehow that seemed wrong.

"Is Lucky all right?"

It was Bee, sitting against the wall of the station on a once-green bench like the one inside.

I sighed.

"They won't let me see him."

She got up and stood beside me, one hand on my arm.

"It's almost time for the evening service."

"Right. Of course. Thank you. I'd completely . . ."

"Why don't we walk together. You can tell me about it on the way."

So I had my chariot follow us back to the parsonage. I filled her in on what had happened there, the arrest, and my conversation with Chief Tho.

"I was bluffing when I said that. I have no idea whether my right to use the Book of Deeds extends to Lucky. But I hoped the chief didn't either."

"I've heard of it, but I don't really know what it *is* or how you use it."

"*You* don't use it. They call in a reader—a special office of the clergy—who brings a Bible with access, and he calls up the record of whatever time and person is being investigated."

"And reads that to the court?"

"Not exactly. The term 'reader' is a bit of a misnomer, or maybe that's what they did a long time ago; I don't really know. But now he displays it for the whole court, like those morality dramas Bibles display for the unchosen."

"So if Lucky had the reader display what he was doing at the time of the murder, it would prove him innocent?"

"Provided that he is, yes. But I wasn't counting on that."

"Why not?"

"Mostly because I wasn't thinking that far ahead."

"What *were* you counting on?"

"I thought the chief was bluffing. I'm almost certain that he planted that police rod in Lucky's room, which would mean that he's trying to blame Lucky—"

"—which means he doesn't really think he did it!"

"Exactly. He's just using this to put pressure on me to turn over these mysterious books. I figured if he knew I was willing to have the Book of Deeds read in court, then he would realize his bluff wasn't working and let Lucky go, but . . ."

"But?"

"But it didn't work. He may have more against Lucky than he's saying."

Her eyes narrowed.

"You still think Lucky could be a murderer?"

"I don't know *what* to think."

Chapter 16

"Consider the society as a whole as two circles intersecting each other—a Venn diagram. One circle represents that part which is governed by the society's norms: its laws, its worldview, its religious habits. The other circle is the part which is suppressed—beliefs and behaviors the society deems illegal or immoral, unconventional or threatening. The intersection is a territory—physical or social or intellectual—where the two can coexist. Every society has these places, for a variety of reasons."

Dorothy Kenning, *The Short Domination: A Student Primer*

IT WAS warm that evening after the service. I took my time closing up the sanctuary and walking back to the parsonage. I wasn't in any hurry to rush home to an empty house. As I approached I noticed there were no lights on. I should have been expecting that, of course. No Lucky, no lights, no evening meal prepared. No conversation over the meal. And Lucky, in the village, sitting alone in a cell. I wondered if they'd let me bring him a meal from the Humble Monk. Even if they wouldn't let me see him, they might pass some food to him.

Bee was waiting for me by the kitchen door.

"Get changed," she said. "We're going out to dinner."

"We are?"

"Don't argue. Just put on some street clothes. Nothing too dressy."

"Too dressy?"

"Just change."

So I left her in the living room and went upstairs to change. Another evening I might have insisted on knowing what she had in mind, but anywhere with company—especially Bee's company—seemed preferable to that empty house.

When I came down she took my arm and said we could walk there.

"Where?"

"You'll see."

She guided us through parts of the village that I rarely visited, though they weren't so different from my own neighborhood. The same picket fences, the same rose bushes, the same golden streets with the same statues of Joshua standing sentry on the corners.

Eventually I realized we were getting close to squatter territory, and I slowed our pace.

"Where exactly are you taking me?"

"We're almost there."

We turned a corner and she pointed across the street, at a clapboard building. The door was standing open and light streamed into the street. The sign above the door wasn't lit at all, and I could just make out the name of the place.

THE THIRSTY ANGEL

I stopped walking.

"What exactly were you planning to do here?"

"Have dinner. It's a restaurant."

I scowled.

She grinned and added, "Well, it serves food anyway."

She pulled at my arm, but I didn't move. I was remembering her attempt to steal the Lazarus Stone.

"Listen, Bee. I'm not going in there unless I know exactly what you're planning."

"I'm not *planning* anything. I just thought it would be a good idea to get a look at the place where Lucky and that murdered man were meeting."

"And?"

"And nothing. You hadn't planned anything for dinner, right?"

"I hadn't actually thought about it."

"And Lucky couldn't plan it, as he usually would, because—"

"He's in jail."

"Exactly," she said. "So we both need to eat."

"*And . . .*"

"And the more we know about what was going on, the better our chance of helping Lucky."

"I thought so."

"I'm not planning anything other than a meal."

"You promise?"

THE OPEN DOOR WAS DECEPTIVE. It opened onto a short hallway, guarded by a hefty man just inside. He was several inches taller than me, and wore a sort of vest over a loose shirt, open at the collar. He hadn't shaved recently.

He bowed to us as we entered, with a bit of a flourish.

"Welcome to the Thirsty Angel, Pastor. It isn't often we have the honor of a visit from a man of the cloth!"

He beamed a generous smile at Bee. His teeth were yellow and a bit crooked.

"Nor," he continued, "such a charming lady!"

Bee accepted the compliment with the same tilt of the head and smile she would have granted a holder.

He stuck a rough hand out to me.

"Gabriel Hauser, Pastor. The proprietor of this establishment. Will the two of you be dining with us this evening?"

"We'd hoped to."

"Well then, your hopes will not be in vain. I see the lady is not carrying her Bible. If you'll just allow me to take charge of yours, I'll arrange for a table."

"My Bible?"

"Yes sir."

He pointed toward a sign that hung on the wall behind us. It read:

NO POLICE.

NO WEAPONS.

NO BIBLES.

ALL GUESTS WILL CONDUCT THEMSELVES

WITH DECORUM AT ALL TIMES,

AND CHEERFULLY ACCEDE

TO ANY REQUEST FROM THE STAFF.

-THE MANAGEMENT.

"Policy, sir."

"I've never heard of such a thing."

"I'm sure you haven't, Pastor. Not traveling in the circles

you're used to. But as the saying goes, 'When you're roaming, roam as the roamers do'."

He held out his hand.

"I'll take good care of it. I promise."

I handed it to him and he nodded his approval. He placed it on a high shelf with a few others, and gestured for us to go ahead of him toward the dining area.

The word 'dining' was almost certainly an exaggeration, though the room was heavy with the scent of food. It was large, with wooden floors and a high ceiling. The walls were decorated with various used signs—some of them were street signs, some had once hung outside a business, some just sported lettered aphorisms.

Some of those I had heard before, others I hadn't, and still others I didn't even understand.

There was no music, just the noise of plates and silverware and loud conversation. Everyone seemed to be trying to be heard above everyone else. Waiters rushed from one table to the next delivering food and drink. The smaller tables around the edges of the room held couples—eating, drinking, playing chess or cards or some kind of dice game. There was even one man actually reading a book—not a Bible, but a real book like the ones that had caused me so much trouble. No one seemed to notice.

Our host waved to a waiter—a small, ancient fellow with bright eyes—and he came bustling over.

"Show these guests to our best table, Henry."

Henry nodded to us, and led the way. The best table turned out to be the one by the door to the kitchen.

He pulled Bee's chair out, and held it while she seated herself.

She gave him the same smile between equals that she had given me at the Humble Monk.

"Thank you, Henry."

He sent a furtive glance toward the proprietor, who was returning to his station at the door, then addressed us in a confidential tone.

"Just between us, there is no 'best table'. He says that to everyone."

Bee gave me an amused glance.

Henry continued. "So will the two of you be eating with us, or are you just here for drinks?"

"We're here for dinner," I said, "but how are we supposed to consult your menu without a Bible?"

He stifled a chuckle.

"There's no menu at the Angel. I can list the drinks for you —there's only three. And dinner is dinner. Tonight it's corn chowder."

"So the drinks?"

"Beer, wine, and gin. Tonight's wine is red."

I raised my eyebrows at Bee.

"I think I'll try the beer," she said.

Henry nodded approval.

"That's the safest choice."

"I'll have the same then, Henry."

And he toddled off.

Bee surveyed the room with relish.

"Isn't this delicious?"

"It's certainly different."

"And Lucky was coming here regularly?"

"He was gone so often in the evenings I thought he had a girl-friend."

"Look at that."

She pointed to a small house, hanging on the wall across the room from us.

It was carved out of wood, complete with a roof, a little tower above the roof, trees growing to either side of the house, and windows in the second story—above where the front door would have been. But instead of a door, there was a circle with numbers on it and two little arrows pointing at the numbers. Two brass pine-cones, completely out of scale, hung below it, and a wooden branch with carved leaves swung back and forth behind them.

I had never seen anything like it, yet it seemed strangely familiar.

"What do you think it is?" I said.

Bee nodded toward a table in the corner.

"Have you noticed what that fellow's doing?"

"Reading a book."

"I think we're in the kind of place that doesn't pay much attention to the rules. I suspect that thing on the wall is a clock."

"Right out in the open like that?"

"That's my guess."

I pushed my chair back.

"We should probably leave."

"Why would we leave? You have to admit we're learning stuff we didn't know about Lucky."

"I'm a pastor, Bee. I shouldn't be in a place like this."

"Joshua consorted with publicans and sinners."

"Yes. Well, Joshua didn't have to explain himself to his denomination."

She gave me a mischievous smile.

"So what you really mean is you can't be *caught* in a place like this."

"At the very least."

"Let me ask you something. Who's the most likely person in this room to report that book over there?"

I searched one face after another. None of them seemed to even be interested.

"I don't know."

"I do. It was a real question."

"Who, then?"

"You."

I gave her a grudging smile. She continued.

"And are you going to?"

I pulled my chair back to the table.

"No," I said. "I'm not."

Henry returned with our beers. He gave us a knowing wink as he planted them on the table.

"It's a beauty, isn't it?"

"What is?" I asked.

"Our clock. I saw you two admiring it."

"How long has it been there?"

"Forever. The table just below it is where they used to sit."

"They?"

"Will and Lucky. He works for you, doesn't he? Lucky?"

"How did you know that?"

"I'm right, ain't I?"

Bee lifted her glass toward him.

"You're an observant man, Henry."

"And I draw conclusions, as well."

"What sort of conclusions did you draw about Lucky and his friend?"

"I wouldn't call them friends, exactly."

"No?"

"More like friendly adversaries, I suppose. They weren't enemies, exactly, but they seemed to be using each other. And both of them was hiding something, too."

"What did they talk about?"

"Books."

"Books?"

"Not in general, mind. Certain books in particular. Will thought Lucky could help him find them, and Lucky claimed not to know anything about them. Lucky wanted Will to tell him why they were important, and Will wouldn't or couldn't. I'll be back with your chowder."

He disappeared into the kitchen.

Bee shot me a look of triumph.

"Glad we came?"

Henry was back before I could respond. He plopped a bowl of chowder in front of each of us, glanced over his shoulder to make sure the proprietor wasn't watching, and continued with his conclusions.

"I figure neither one believed the other. That's why they kept coming back. Lucky didn't believe Will could be so interested in finding those books if he didn't know why they were important, and Will didn't believe Lucky would be so interested in why they were important if he'd never heard of them. Enjoy your meal."

He vanished again, leaving us to taste the chowder.

It wasn't bad.

Chapter 17

Albert Ransom, in his inaugural address
to the New College of Ancient History

"THERE's A LIMIT, you know, to what I can do."

Boyd stood on the edge of a rise overlooking his wheat
fields at the west end of the Valley. It was going to be a hot day.
The scent of baked chaparral hung in the air. The harvest was
late that year, and the cherubim were still moving through the
fields below.

They were too far from us to be terrifying, but I still found
an eerie and unsettling fascination in the flurry of wings and

wheels and eyes and faces, silently devouring the standing wheat and leaving sacks of grain stacked in their wake.

I understood why we had not been allowed on this part of the estate as children. To have glimpsed a cherub when I was just a boy—instead of seeing that guardian angel—would have left a far different mark on my soul.

I had half-expected Boyd's response—even though Lucky had been an unofficial uncle to both of us. The burden of the Franklyn holdings had worked its changes on Boyd, even in the relatively brief time since he'd inherited.

"I understand," I said. "But there must be something."

He frowned at the scene below, then turned to face me.

"I can't think what. I don't have direct authority over the police, you know, or over the judge. I might have a bit of influence, but not enough to interfere with a murder investigation."

"We're talking about Lucky, Boyd. We can't just stand by."

"I agree with the sentiment wholeheartedly. But as a practical matter . . . How much evidence is there?"

"That's the thing. Almost none." I listed it for him. "Dennis wouldn't have arrested him without more, but Chief Tho took over, and—"

"And found the murder weapon in his room."

"Or planted it there."

"And why would he do that?"

"There could be a lot of reasons. Maybe Tho was involved. Maybe he's protecting someone. Maybe he has it in for Lucky."

"It sounds like you're grasping at straws, even to *me*."

"Then why wouldn't he allow Lucky to consult the Book of Deeds? He obviously doesn't want the truth to be uncovered."

Boyd nodded.

"It's a point. But there could be—as you say—many reasons. Knowing Tho, I wouldn't be surprised if he refused you just to pull rank."

I started to object, but he cut me off.

"Look Adam, I've got an estate to run, and part of that depends upon a good relationship with the police. I can't accuse Tho of framing Lucky based on mere speculation. It would destroy the goodwill I need from that quarter, and it wouldn't do Lucky any good either. You don't have any evidence."

"But neither do they."

"They've got the weapon, planted or not. They've got the fact that he lied about knowing the victim, and that's according to your detective friend—unless you think *he* can't be trusted?"

"No."

"Is that *all* they have?"

"As far as I know. Dennis would have told me if there were more."

"Then they still have more than you do. You need an alternative story—something solid, with at least a little evidence behind it."

"Where am I going to get that by this afternoon?"

"Your best bet is to get Lucky to tell you whatever he knows, so you have something to go on."

"I would, if they'd just let me see him, but they won't."

MY FIRST INSTINCT, when I saw him, was to just slip away as quickly and quietly as possible. I had spent the entire morning after my unsuccessful chat with Boyd racking my brain for some way to postpone Lucky's hearing, to pull strings to save him, or at the very least to get in to see him. Bee had disappeared, so I had been on my own, and I hadn't come up with a thing.

I found myself in the doorway of the Humble Monk only because it was a Thursday and that's what I did on Thursdays.

Pure habit. Presbyter Brine hadn't crossed my mind since Lucky's arrest—any more than anything else had.

Yet there he was, waiting for me, expecting me to show up with those damn books.

I took a step backward and half-closed the door before I thought better of it. I needed to pull some strings, and Brine might be able to help. I didn't have his precious books, and I didn't much care whether he fired or promoted me, but Lucky was a different matter. I'd take whatever help I could get, and pay whatever price I had to pay.

I went inside.

Brine looked me up and down as I approached, obviously hoping I was carrying a package.

I took the seat across from him and didn't wait for small talk.

"Presbyter Brine, I need a favor, and I don't have much time."

He smiled at me.

"Delighted, my boy. That's what we of the cloth are here for. To serve. Is it about your . . . ahhh . . . employee? I hear he's in a bit of trouble."

"He didn't commit this crime, sir. But the local authorities are intent on getting him executed. I have to find a way to save him, and I only have a few hours."

"I'm sure he didn't. And as for the authorities . . . there are, well, *ways and means,* you understand. Almost anything, if approached with the . . . ahhh . . . the proper leverage . . ."

"You can do it then? Save him?"

"Oh, certainly. Of course these matters can be a bit complex. If you could just . . . just assure me that I am mistaken . . ."

"Mistaken?"

"I couldn't help noticing . . . or rather *not* noticing, I suppose . . . the package that we spoke of at our last . . ."

"Oh, that. I haven't had any time to even think about it with

Lucky's arrest. I'd even forgotten our meeting until I saw you through the door."

"I'm relieved to hear it. So the lack of any package doesn't mean...?"

"I need to be frank with you, sir."

"Yes?"

"I would do almost anything to save Lucky. I would gladly give you the—the items in question. But I've been telling you the absolute truth. I don't have them. The most I can do is promise you that if you save Lucky and I ever do have them, I will give them to you immediately."

The waiter served Brine's meal, then turned to me.

"What can I get you, Pastor?"

I waved him away.

"Nothing for me."

Brine ate for a long time in silence. It was as though I wasn't even there. Finally he wiped his lips with a napkin and gave me an appraising stare.

"It pains me to ... there are two ... ahhh ... difficulties I face regarding your—"

"Friend."

"Yes. Of course. Your friend."

"Difficulties?"

"The first is a matter of trust. You almost convince me ... indeed, your anxiety over the plight of your ... ahhh ... your friend almost convinces me that you are telling the truth. But only *almost*."

"What would it take to—"

"The second difficulty is pragmatic. I mentioned, earlier, the need of the proper leverage, you'll recall ..."

He took another bite of his food, and chewed thoughtfully.

"Yes," I said. "I recall."

"Um?"

"Leverage."

"Ahhh. Well, unfortunately for all of us . . . that is, for you, for your friend, and, I'm afraid, for me as well . . . Unfortunately, the leverage I would need would be the . . . ahhh . . . the very items in question."

"I see."

"So, your inability—honest or not—your inability to produce them . . . I'm afraid . . ."

<hr>

"MUST BE NICE, having friends in high places."

Dennis took a sip of his coffee and knitted his brows at me.

"Do I?"

He grinned.

"You know you do. We had a visit from the holder this morning. He was in the chief's office for about twenty minutes."

"And?"

"You get to see Lucky, the hearing's been postponed to Saturday afternoon, and it's possible Lucky's going to be allowed a reading when the hearing does happen."

I breathed a sigh of relief.

Dennis took another sip.

"Don't get your hopes up on that last one," he said. "It's not in the bag yet."

"But I can see Lucky?"

"I'll take you down when we're through here. It's not all good news, you know."

"Tell me."

"That rod that the chief found—"

"—that the chief *pretended* to find—"

"—it's not a regulation rod. It's a different weight, the grip at the end is circular rather than oval, and it's a lot more powerful."

"Powerful enough to leave that hole in his chest?"

"Probably. We haven't finished the testing. But it's definitely enough to kill him. So the question would be where Lucky could get such a thing."

"Or where Tho would."

"That's not going to get you anywhere. If you want to help Lucky, concentrate on helping Lucky. Going after the chief isn't going to do it."

LUCKY'S CELL was in the basement, not far from the room where Dennis had shown me the body and I had discovered the fake logo. It was a small room with a peephole in the door, a narrow bench built along the back wall, and a single monkstone panel set into the ceiling to provide heat and dim light. There was no antiseptic in the air, only dampness and a slight whiff of mold.

Lucky sat on the bench, next to his Bible. He looked up as Dennis let me in and closed the door behind me.

"Good to see you, Lad."

"Do you need anything? I don't know what they'll let me bring, but . . ."

"I'm fine. Thanks for bringing my Bible."

"I'm really sorry about this, Lucky."

He shrugged.

"Not your fault, near as I can see."

"No, but I'm doing everything I can to get you out of here. I know you didn't do it."

"That makes exactly two of us, then."

"More than that. Bee's helping me, Boyd got me in to see you, and he got your hearing postponed to give us time. It isn't going to be easy. You didn't tell the truth about knowing Will Terren, and they *know* you didn't—"

"That was stupid. I panicked."

"They found the weapon in your room—"

"It wasn't mine. They put it there themselves."

"That's exactly what I think, but it's still evidence against you, unless we can prove otherwise. That's why I'm here. We've got to come up with a better theory at the very least. Or some evidence that you're innocent. So I need you to tell me everything you know."

"That's not much."

"You knew Will Terren."

"Just barely. He approached me in town one day. Said we might be able to help each other out. I asked how. He offered to buy me a beer while he explained."

"And you agreed?"

"Yeah. It sounded fishy, and I almost didn't meet him, but..."

"But...?"

He cracked a smile.

"It was a free beer."

"Lucky."

"I wanted to know what it was about. It had to be about you in some way. No one was going to be interested in me for any other reason. I wanted to find out what he was up to."

"Did you?"

He wrinkled his brow and shook his head.

"He wanted to know about some books you had. He thought for sure that I would know about them, or be able to find out. He wouldn't say more than that, but he wanted to meet again. I kept hoping to get more out of him—more about the books themselves, about why he thought you had them, or about why he was so interested in them. I guess he must have come to the parsonage that evening looking for them."

"And you don't know who killed him?"

"Like I told the police, when I got to the top of the stairs he was already lying there."

"It's very little to go on."

"It's got to do with the police chief. He sneaked the weapon into my room. Why would he do that, unless he's involved in some way? I'd try to find out where he got that rod from."

"I'll do that."

"I'm not the only innocent person he's arrested, you know. Remember that woman who was executed last week? She may have been involved."

"Really? I can't imagine how."

"You should see what you can find out about her, Lad."

Chapter 18

David Kinde (ancestor of Adam Kinde)

BEE WAS WAITING on the bench by the wall when I came out.

"Dennis said Boyd got you in to see him."

"He did."

"And he got the hearing postponed, as well."

I nodded.

"It gives us a little time."

"Do you have a plan? Because I do."

"You do?"

"We need to find out everything we can before the trial, find something that will either prove he didn't do it, or that someone else could have. That's what I think, anyway. What's your plan?"

I chuckled.

"Let's go with yours. Lucky gave me two ideas. He suggested that we try to find out who made the fake police rod they found in his room, and he suggested that we try to find out more about that woman who was executed last week."

"Which do you want to do first?"

"The police rod. It makes sense, especially if we can prove that it was made for Tho. The only reason I can see for finding out about that woman is that Lucky asked me to. I doubt if she had anything to do with this."

"He must have had his reasons. And he's the one who would be executed."

"And I think we should look into her for that reason. I'm just saying she shouldn't be our first priority."

Bee frowned.

"So how would we go about tracking down the person who made the rod?"

"Off the top of my head? I haven't a clue."

"Because," she said, "I do have an idea how to track down that woman."

"Really?"

"That's what I spent the morning doing."

I HAD NEVER HAD occasion to venture so far into squatter territory during the short time I had been pastor. There were ways in which it was similar to the village: the grid of streets and blocks was the same, and the Franklyns had probably commissioned the same monastery for the statues of Joshua on every corner.

But the streets were dirt, not golden; the sidewalks were

almost completely gone; and the few pieces that remained from the Dark Age tilted at odd angles.

The houses were a hodge-podge of ancient walls—where they had somehow survived the termites—and makeshift barriers of woven branches or adobe brick, crammed together, sometimes touching, sometimes leaning on each other in order to remain standing.

Bee had apparently drawn the same conclusion as Lucky, though with a bit more information to go on. She hadn't told me everything about her conversation with the squatter she'd met that morning we visited Anna. He was the brother of the woman who had been executed, and when he'd seen that Bee was a holder, he had appealed to her for help. He told her that the real wrongdoer had been Tho—that the trial had been a way to get rid of his sister because she was a witness to Tho's crimes.

Bee thought that sounded very close to Lucky's situation, and had spent the morning tracking down the woman's family based on what little the squatter had told her, what she'd been able to wheedle out of the desk sergeant, and information from several other sources I didn't even know she had.

I still thought we were wasting our time, even if Lucky and Bee outvoted me. There was no concrete connection between Lucky and the executed woman, while the fake police rod was both tangible and connected. But I didn't have any ideas about how to research the rod.

In spite of Bee's morning labors we found the place mostly by a combination of wandering around and asking questions. I wouldn't have gotten far on my own. At least half the women we saw were dressed exactly like the men, with just the short skirt and either bare feet or sandals. Bee had to force me to approach any of them for directions.

Squatter territory was dry, above all else. There was none of the lush greenery that surrounded my life in the village. No lawns, few trees, and even they had leaves more brown than green. The greenest parts were the vegetable gardens, laid out in neat rows of dry dirt. Hollow sticks stuck out of the ground at the base of every plant, and once or twice we saw children carefully measuring water into the tops of those tubes.

I was surprised to find them so willing to be helpful. Everyone we asked stopped whatever they were doing and tried their best to help. When they couldn't, they expressed real regret, and would then suggest where we might try next.

At first I though they were just being polite because of my status as pastor. But when we came across a man who did know the family, he insisted on escorting us there—even though he had only one good leg and the journey took him over an hour. I offered him a coin as an expression of thanks, but he refused—and even seemed a bit injured by my gesture.

Our guide had taken us to a lot in the middle of a block and told us Lucy's sister lived at the very back. We made our way down the side of an older, larger, building and past several other structures to find it. A goat was tethered between two of them, and chickens pecked at the ground in the sunlight between the buildings. There was a meager vegetable garden on the other side.

A woman sat on a stump next to the doorway. She was young—perhaps eighteen or twenty—and the natural attractiveness of youth managed to shine even through the usual squatter gauntness. Her hair was blond and long, flowing down around her bare shoulders. Aside from her hair she wore nothing at all.

As soon as I saw her I stopped and backed away, but Bee grabbed my arm and held it firmly.

The woman was absorbed by her work, which was of a kind I had never seen. She held her left hand a little above eye level, palm down, with a bunch of animal fur lying on the back of it. Her fingers and thumb held one end of a string. At the other end of the string hung a stick with a round flat weight at the bottom. Her right hand alternated between pulling on the top of the string and twisting the stick to keep it spinning.

It took me a moment to realize that she was turning the fur into a sort of yarn, pulling it out little by little and allowing the spinning weight to twist it into a string. When the weight almost touched the ground, she stopped to wrap the excess around the stick and hook it through a notch at the top again, now closer to her hand, so she could spin the next bit.

While she was doing that, she saw us watching her. A combination of fear and defiance crossed her face.

"I'm not doing anything wrong, Pastor. It's only one part moving, as you can see."

I nodded, keeping my eyes on hers.

Bee stepped forward and stuck out a hand.

"Of course you aren't. I'm Beth Raven. Are you by any chance Kate Ford?"

She eyed us suspiciously in silence, but Bee left her hand sticking out the whole time, and finally the woman shook it.

"What do you want with me?"

"We need your help."

It took her a moment to digest that, then she nodded knowingly.

"This is about Lucy, isn't it?"

THE ROOM she lived in was perhaps ten or twelve feet square. The lower six feet of the rear wall was cinder-block, like the wall around the parsonage garden. Above that, it had been extended upwards a foot or so by a combination of woven branches and dried mud. The other walls were adobe, and the floor was packed earth.

The doorway was hung with a loosely knitted fabric,

pushed to one side to let light in since there were no windows. There was a small indentation in the floor, scooped out like a bowl, just inside next to the doorway.

Aside from two small sleeping pads—covered with the same fabric as hung at the door—and a larger one against the opposite wall, the only furniture was a simple altar, barely large enough to heat the room. The gray gloss of monkstone looked completely out of place in those primitive surroundings. Two naked children squatted on the floor in front of it, watching a morality drama unfold in the air between themselves and the altar.

Kate picked the Bible off its perch on the altar and thrust it at one of the children.

"You can watch the rest outside. Go, now."

She pulled a basket from the single shelf on the wall and perused its contents. A simple dress, woven from the same fabric, hung from a hook on the wall, but she made no move to put it on. It was probably the dress she wore to church. A small animal—the size of a squirrel or rat—hung skinned and cleaned from another hook.

"I don't have much in store at the moment. Would you like some nettle tea?"

"Thank you," I said, "but—"

"Yes, please," Bee said. "How kind."

Kate poured water from a clay jug into a small tin—full of dents both large and small, with a wooden stick lashed to it for a handle. She set it on the cooking surface of the altar to heat. While she was waiting for it to boil, she began to talk.

She was the sister of Lucy Ford—the executed woman—and felt, as Lucy's brother had, that a grave injustice had been done.

"You can't tell anyone—anyone in the village—that I'm the one who told you."

I thought we might need her for a witness, but Bee answered before I could speak.

"We promise. No one will know but us."

So she told us her story.

Water was hard to come by for squatters, who had no money to pay for it and no patron to supply it for free. There were no free water lines under the streets providing an endless supply, as there were in the village. And they needed more than the villagers, because their gardens and their animals were their only sources of food.

But the Franklyns had always been generous, even to squatters. The water chariots came by regularly, squirting a basic ration into the cisterns of various shapes and sizes the people provided.

The Franklyn company supplied the water, but not the delivery. That was left to the fire department, which already had the water chariots and the staff to deal with them.

The fire department was a division of the police department, which meant that Tho was in charge. Under his supervision the water rations had dwindled over the years, to the point where there was barely enough to live on.

When Lucy's husband became ill and died, her water ration was cut by more than half, even though her sister was living with her and she still had two children to support.

The neighbors were supportive, but they had barely enough for themselves, so finally, in desperation, Lucy complained to Tho.

Tho offered her a way to earn more water.

She was still young and attractive, and he had certain "important friends" that he wished to entertain when they visited the village. If she refused, her water rations could be cut further, or perhaps one of her children would be caught stealing. On the other hand, if she cooperated she could have her water rations restored, and even some food from the village for herself and her children.

She had agreed, but she'd hated what she had to do.

Then, a week before her death, she'd told Kate that she wasn't going to have to do it much longer.

"Lucy wouldn't say why, just that she had a way to make Papa Tho let her go, and let her keep fair rations as well. I told her she was crazy if she thought she could force him to do anything. I begged her to tell me what she was going to do. But she wouldn't."

"She gave you no hint at all?"

"She wouldn't tell me anything. Said it was too dangerous for me to know. And then she was arrested, and they tried her, and . . ."

There was a tear in her eye and her chin began to tremble. But when she looked up she was angry.

"He *has* to pay for that."

I wanted to promise her that he would, but I had no idea how I could keep that promise.

Bee took a different tack.

"Kate," she said, "your sister wasn't the only one, was she?"

"No," Kate mused, "but I don't know who the others were. Except . . ."

"Except?"

"Except for one. Her name was Rose. I don't know her or her last name, but sometimes Tho would send a chariot to pick them up together, and Rose would come here to wait for it."

"We came to you," Bee said, "because Tho is trying to kill a friend of ours, just like he did Lucy. We don't have much time, but if we could talk to Rose it might help us stop him from getting our friend executed, and it might even help us make him pay for what he did to Lucy."

"I'd like to help, but that's really all I know."

"Do you think you could find out? We don't know squatter

territory. We could spend a year looking and still never find her. But you might be able to find her in time."

"I don't know. I have to think of Lucy's kids. If Tho found out I was looking for her . . ."

"Maybe you could think of a reason to look for her. One that even Tho wouldn't object to?"

She thought about that, then shook her head.

"I don't know what—wait."

She went to the large sleeping mat and lifted a corner on the wall side. She pulled out a brooch. It was handcrafted jewelry, brightly colored, in the shape of a blossom. She held it out for our inspection in the palm of her hand.

"I found this after Lucy was arrested. I think Tho gave it to her, to wear when she . . . but I could say I thought it was Rose's, that I was looking for Rose to return it."

She cupped the brooch in both hands and nodded to herself.

"Yes. I could do that."

Chapter 19

"Guilt and shame are fundamental tools of power. Humans will go to great lengths to avoid or deny either. Offer a way out, and they will embrace it. The trick is to bury the source so deeply that it appears inescapable."

The Chief Servant, in an address to the Select Committee, on the eve of the Council of Columbia

KATE TOOK us to see her brother on our way out, but he had nothing to add to what he had told Bee on the road to the Franklyn Estate that day. He thought Lucy had been killed to keep her from telling something she knew, and he based his belief on the same information Kate had.

None of this dampened Bee's spirits at all. She was confident we were on the right track, and filled with optimism on our long walk back to the village.

"We're going to fix this. I know it."

"I wish I were as certain. I'm not sure what any of this has to do with Lucky—or the murder, for that matter."

"We don't have all the facts yet, but it's all connected somehow."

"Maybe."

A large crow flapped its way from one tree to another. There was a distant burst of laughter from a nearby building. I thought I detected a whiff of woodsmoke in the air.

"It's just so encouraging, don't you think? To see how kind these people are, in spite of their poverty?"

"Let's not get into that again. You don't want to believe that we're all fallen. Fine. Just don't ask me to talk about it."

"But surely what you've seen today gives you pause? That man who spent an hour of his day helping us find Lucy's family, just to be nice? And he wouldn't take a single coin from you. Do you know how much money that was to a squatter, who might never own a single coin in his life? Or what about Kate, taking care of Lucy's children, and willing to risk Tho's wrath to help us help Lucky?"

"Yes. Tho. There's your example of the goodness of humanity."

"But that's the point. He's the exception, not the rule."

"And what about Lucy? Fornicating for water."

"Don't tell me you're going to blame *her* for that."

"I'm just saying, she was committing a sin. Violating her own purity. And don't say she didn't have a choice."

"Of course she had a choice, and she chose to protect her family, at great cost to herself. Almost any woman would."

"By prostituting herself? I doubt that. I'd bet a great many women would have resisted."

"And a great many would have made her sacrifice."

"What does that say about women? And what about her sister?"

"What about her sister?"

"You saw her. Parading around naked, and in front of her pastor. Shameless."

"Shameless?"

She smiled at that.

"So she lacked shame, and you take that as evidence that she has a fallen nature?"

"I'm just saying that she clearly has no sense of decency, of right and wrong."

"Of good and evil?"

"Yes. Of basic morality."

Bee was silent for a long time then, and I began to think I might have overstated my case.

"Look, I'm not saying she's any worse than any of us. That's my point. We're *all* fallen—it's human nature. That's why we need rules, morality, to keep us in line."

I was fairly sure that hadn't made anything better. We trudged on in silence for a while, then Bee spoke again.

"You don't have a clue why you're so married to this idea, do you?"

"It's a doctrine, actually."

"Why you're so attached to this *doctrine*, then."

"I suppose you're going to tell me."

"Because it's the most important doctrine in your theology."

"Hardly. I'd say there are much more important doctrines."

"Such as?"

"Such as the divinity of Joshua, for one."

"And why is that important?"

"Because he came to save us."

"Save us from . . .?"

"It doesn't really matter which doctrine is more important. What matters is that it's true. You can't avoid it. It's right there at the very beginning of the scriptures."

"Adam and Eve, you mean?"

"It's undeniable."

"So you think that story actually happened, in real life, just as it's described there?"

I was shocked.

"You need to be careful, Bee. You're perilously close to heresy."

"By suggesting that you could take the story more seriously?"

"It sounds more like you're suggesting that I shouldn't take it seriously at all."

Her face scrunched in thought.

"Okay. Let's say this. Say you asked me if I was hungry, and I replied that I could eat a horse. Would I be taking your question seriously?"

"Well, it would be a rather light-hearted way of responding—"

"Yes. It would. But would it be taking *your question* seriously? Taking it to mean exactly what it meant?"

"I guess so. Yes. It would."

"So let's say you that you responded by suggesting that neither the Humble Monk nor the Thirsty Angel served horse meat, and in any case a whole horse would be more than anyone could eat in a single meal. Would you be taking *my answer* seriously?"

"I'd just be joking."

"Right. But would that joke be taking my response to your question seriously? Would it be taking my response to mean exactly what it meant?"

"What has this got to do with Adam and Eve?"

"Would it?"

"No. I would be pretending that you were speaking literally when I knew full well that you were using a figure of speech."

"And how would you know that 'full well'?"

I thought about that for a moment.

"Context, I suppose, and the fact that what you described was impossible."

"Okay. So tell me the story of Adam and Eve."

"Well, Adam and Eve live in this garden. And there are two trees in the garden. The tree of life, and the tree of knowledge—"

"Let's take those one at a time, and just use a bit of common sense. If I told you I had a tree of apples in my garden, what fruit would you say grew on the tree?"

"Apples."

"And if I said 'a tree of pears'?"

"Pears."

"So it would be reasonable to suppose that the fruit of the tree of life would be . . ."

"Life. Yes. Perfectly orthodox. In fact, later in the story it says that if they ate the fruit of the tree of life they would live forever."

"But I think you've misnamed the other tree."

"Not misnamed, exactly. Just shortened. But you're right. It's actually the tree of the knowledge of good and evil."

"And so the 'fruit' of that tree would be the knowledge of good and evil?"

"Yes."

"And God tells them not to eat it?"

"Yes."

"Does he give a reason?"

"He says that if they eat it they will die."

"And do they?"

"Do they what?"

"Die?"

"They're banned from the garden. It's a spiritual death."

"So they're living in this garden, and what happens next?"

"Well, a serpent approaches Eve, and tempts her to eat the apple."

"So there's an apple tree in the garden as well?"

"You know what I meant—the fruit of the tree of the knowledge of good and evil."

"So he tempts her to learn about good and evil."

"Again. Perfectly orthodox. In fact, it says right in the text that she's tempted because she thinks it will make her wise."

"So, at this point in the story we have two trees—one whose fruit is life itself, one whose fruit is a deadly form of knowledge —and a talking snake, yes?"

"Yes."

"Do snakes talk?"

"Well, not in general, but—"

"And do trees like that exist, anywhere in your experience?"

"Not now, but this was long ago.

"Really? Do you really believe that there was a time when the world was filled with talking snakes, and with trees that bore life and knowledge in the form of fruit?"

"But this is scripture. It's the Word of God."

"Exactly. And if you believe that, don't you think you should take it *seriously*?"

"But that's what I'm saying."

"No. You're saying you take it *literally*. It's like pretending I would really like to eat a horse. The story is screaming at you that it's *not* literal. It's full of talking snakes and trees with fruit that isn't apples or anything like any fruit in the real world. How did you say you would know I didn't really mean I could eat a horse?"

"Because it would be impossible."

She nodded.

I relented.

"So maybe—just maybe—the story's not intended to be literal. Okay."

"What does the name 'Adam' mean?"

"It's Hebrew for 'man,' or 'human'."

"And 'Eve'?"

"It's Hebrew for 'living'. The passage explains that by saying it's because she is the mother of all living."

"So it might just be another way of saying 'woman'?"

"Possibly. But even if Adam and Eve just represent all men and women, it still says the same thing—maybe even more so. We all disobey God, we all sin, we're all banned from life because of it."

"And what is that sin?"

"What do you mean?"

"Is it murder, or lying, or stealing, or what? What did Eve do that she was warned not to do, that would lead to death?"

"She ate the app—she ate the fruit."

"She thought it would be wise to learn about good and evil?"

"Okay."

"And what was the first effect of this sin—the sin of learning about good and evil?"

"They were banned from the—"

"The *first* effect."

I had walked right into it. I sighed.

"They were ashamed—of being naked."

"So they were 'shameless' *before* the fall?"

"Yeah. You're pretty good at turning things around, but—"

"And shame over their nakedness was a sign that they had fallen?"

I was silent. She continued.

"And the sin that led to this was knowing good and evil?"

"Yes."

"And where do people learn about good and evil, about right and wrong?"

"I don't understand."

"I think you do."

"You mean from the, from the scriptures, from the law, I suppose, but—"

"And what did God say about that kind of knowledge?"

"This can't be right. There's got to be—"

"—a loophole? A way out?"

"No. I just mean . . ."

"What did God say?"

"That it led to death. But—"

She grinned at me.

"I think we turn left here. The village isn't very far."

<hr>

WE WERE both exhausted by the time we got back to the village. I almost wished I had broken my own rule and taken my chariot into squatter territory—except that it wouldn't have been at all proper with Bee on board. But it *would* have meant we didn't have time for a very uncomfortable conversation about Adam and Eve.

I asked Bee how she learned to interpret scripture that way, and she said she read a lot of books. I asked which books.

"You wouldn't have seen them."

"Why not?"

"I didn't read them on a Bible. They were in my family's library."

I found myself envying her holder status, and wondering whether the gap between a pastor and a holder could ever really be bridged.

We arrived at the parsonage just before the evening service. Bee suggested we plan our next move over an early breakfast at the Humble Monk.

"I have a better idea," I said, "if you're interested."

"I probably am. What is it?"

"How about another dinner at the Thirsty Angel?"

"Does this have to do with Lucky, or do you just want a cheap date?"

"It's about Lucky."

"Damn."

"Seriously. We've made some progress with Kate, though we still haven't found any real connection there to Lucky's problem. But we haven't done a thing about the fake rod, and that's probably more important."

"And your solution is to have dinner out?"

I smiled in spite of myself. The truth was that I wanted to end our day on a more pleasant note, but I didn't tell her that.

"It occurred to me," I said, "that a man with a clock on his wall might know where we could find a sorcerer."

Chapter 20

———

"And we cannot leave out of the equation countless alliances on the personal level. These quite often occur across the boundaries of class and station."

———

Dorothy Kenning, *The Short Domination: A Student Primer*

"To what do I owe the honor of this invitation?"

Gabriel Hauser beamed his stained-tooth smile at me and then at Bee. He was wearing the same shirt and vest he wore the night before, and he still hadn't shaved.

I had asked him to join us as I handed him my Bible at the entrance. He waved us on in. Henry seated us, brought us each a beer—this time without asking first—and seconds later the proprietor pulled a chair up to our table.

"We were wondering," I said, "whether you could help us out."

"Henry!" he shouted. "A beer!"

He leaned across the table, lowered his voice, and winked at me.

"I can say—with conviction, Pastor—that *that* is almost a certainty. You'll be happy to know that the occasions on which I cannot be of service are rare indeed."

"Well, it's nothing very difficult. You'll either know or you won't. We're just looking for some information."

"For a *connection*, actually," said Bee.

He looked at her with appreciation.

"I have a feeling that the lady may understand these matters better than you do, Pastor."

"A connection then. I'm not sure why it matters what you call it, but—"

"The difference," he said, "is twofold. A connection involves me vouching for both parties to both parties, assuring trust. And since that trust is valuable, it requires a higher consideration."

"Consideration?"

Bee whispered in my ear.

"A fee."

"Exactly," said the proprietor. "A way of showing your appreciation for value provided."

A small door opened at the top of the clock on the wall, and a carving of a bird popped out and called 'whoo-hoo' multiple times.

Bee stuck an elbow in my ribs.

"Oh," I said. "Of course. How much?"

"That would depend entirely on the nature of the connection. On just how difficult, how dangerous, or how secretive it needed to be."

"We need," Bee said, "to find a sorcerer."

He leaned back in his chair and pushed himself away from the table.

"I may have been a bit hasty in my earlier assurances.

Though the occasions upon which I cannot be of service are indeed rare, this is unfortunately one of them."

"But why?"

"Pastor, do you not recall that I have banned Bibles from this establishment?"

"I don't quite see—"

"Why would you think I would have no truck with your magic, and yet would traffic in the magic of others?"

"What have Bibles got to do with—"

"Sorcery, sir? They are both magic."

"But Bibles are miracles, not magic."

He sighed, and took a sip of his beer.

"What do you want with this sorcerer?"

Bee explained about the fake rod, and Lucky's coming hearing. When she was through, he nodded thoughtfully.

"I understand your concern, and even share it to some extent. I have myself a soft spot for Lucky, little as I knew him. But this 'fake' rod. Why do you call it fake?"

Bee just nodded and sat back in her chair. It was up to me to answer.

"Because a real rod is a miracle, wrought in a monastery under the auspices of the church, while this rod was a mere imitation of the authentic thing, created by a sorcerer in violation of God's law."

"I see. And because of that it isn't real?"

"Sorcery provides only an illusion of the real."

"So you wouldn't mind having someone release its power in your direction?"

"Well . . . I wouldn't want to tempt—"

"Come on, pastor. In what sense is this 'fake rod' fake? It looks like a real rod. It feels like a real rod. And it works like a real rod. It was made by a sorcerer, and to my mind that sorcerer isn't so different from one of your monks."

I needed to pull our conversation back to the main point.

"I still don't understand why you can't help us find the sorcerer who made it."

"Because I'll have nothing to do with magic in any form. You see that clock over there? If I wanted, I could take it apart. I could examine its contents, and given time I could explain to you in detail exactly how it does what it does. Can you do that with your Bible?"

"Of course not. It's not the same—"

"Have you ever seen inside a Bible?"

"Yes." I had him there. When a Bible was broken the owner turned it in to me, as pastor, to be issued a new one. I had seen the insides of several Bibles.

"And what did you see?"

"Monkstone."

"All the way through?"

"Yes."

"No moving parts?"

"A Bible isn't clockwork."

"No. It isn't. It's magic, by whatever name you give it. And that clock on the wall, legal or not, is a damn sight more honest than any magic spell."

With that he drained the last of his beer, slammed the empty mug down on the table, and left us.

Bee watched him cross the room.

"That is a very interesting man."

"He may be," I said. "but we're no closer to helping Lucky than when we came in."

The voice came from over my shoulder.

"You got him talking about magic, did you?"

The ancient Henry put our dinners down in front of us. It was onion soup. Apparently the Thirsty Angel only served meals that came in a bowl.

Bee nodded.

"You heard?"

"I wouldn't listen in on a conversation. That wouldn't be polite, ma'am. But magic is the only topic gets him riled like that."

"We asked him if he could put us in touch with a sorcerer."

"That would do it, all right. A shame you didn't know. You could have approached the subject more artfully."

"That would have made a difference?"

"It might've."

"How?"

"Could have asked to be put in touch with a clockmaker. He wouldn't object to that."

"I'm afraid," I said, "that a clockmaker couldn't help us."

"Did Gabriel tell you about taking that clock apart?"

"Yes."

He nodded, and leaned in confidentially.

"Always does, except he never has. Taken it apart, that is. You see, he's only curious on *principle*."

"I'm afraid I don't—"

"I am *pragmatically* curious, though. I *have* taken it apart. And some of the more delicate parts inside are made of monk-stone, or something very like it."

BEE MET me at the parsonage for an early breakfast the next morning. We had little more than a day left until the hearing, and we didn't want to waste a minute of it. I had scrounged the kitchen and come up with some eggs, butter, and blue cheese. There was half a loaf of bread in the bread box, as well.

I had learned to make a pretty good omelet during my last year at seminary, when I had roomed off-campus. That, along with the bread and coffee, made a passable breakfast. Bee was impressed.

We planned out our day as we ate—or as much of it as we

could, anyway. We wanted to follow up on the information we already had, see if that led us any further, and at some point in the day talk to Boyd and visit Lucky again in his cell.

We didn't plan on the knock at my door.

He was clearly a holder. Not a serious working holder like Boyd, but the other type—the kind who merely lived off of his holdings. He was dressed in the latest and most expensive fashion, clothes that Boyd wouldn't have been caught dead in. He sported a monocle, and his walking stick had a diamond-studded handle, which he leaned a gloved hand on while he looked me up and down.

He didn't speak, so I did.

"Hello," I said. "I'm Pastor Adam Kinde. And you are . . .?"

He leaned to one side and peered past me into the living room, where Bee was standing, then gave me an apologetic laugh.

"I'd rather not say, just at the moment. Do you think we could speak in private, Pastor?"

"Is this a spiritual matter? Because I can arrange an appointment for early next week, but at the moment—"

"I don't think even you would classify it as a *spiritual* matter. Personal, perhaps . . ."

He winked at me and continued.

". . . but not spiritual. I have a message for you from a mutual acquaintance of ours."

He winked again and gave a little jerk of his head toward Bee.

"A blossom of sorts. Won't take a moment."

Bee laughed out loud and came to stand beside me.

"You have a message for us from *Rose*?"

The holder managed to look simultaneously shocked and confused. His eyes searched mine for guidance.

"Is that right?" I asked.

He nodded.

I smiled reassuringly.

"You'd better tell us, then."

"She wants to have lunch with you, Pastor. Today, at the Thirsty Angel, she said. She didn't mention the . . . the other lady. Just asked if I could give you the message."

"And you have," Bee said, "just as she asked. Thank you."

He looked from one of us to the other for a moment, then tipped his hat to Bee, nodded to me, and retreated to his waiting chariot without another word.

Chapter 21

"It would be a mistake to assume that the holders lived secure lives. Even though they possessed more wealth and power than could be used in a lifetime of normal pursuits, there were always those among them who were obsessed with increasing both, usually at the expense of their fellows."

Dorothy Kenning, *The Short Domination: A Student Primer*

THE SHOP HAD BEEN in the village since I was a boy, though I'd never been inside.

I expected, when Henry had told us he could connect us to a clockmaker, that we would be going deep into squatter territory again for something so illegal. But the shop opened on the main square, not far from the Humble Monk, and looked no different than the shops around it.

The sign read simply "Simon Fernandez, Woodcarver" and

the window was filled with statues, boxes, frames, doorstops—
anything that could be carved from wood.

It took me about ten seconds to realize why the carving on
the clock at the Thirsty Angel had seemed familiar.

The top of the door bumped a hanging bell as we entered. It
was darker and cooler inside and crowded with displays of his
art. A small man bustled toward us from the back of the shop.
He wore a pair of wire-rimmed glasses and a white apron,
covered with sawdust.

It was the same man who had come to my father's funeral.

"Ah, Pastor Kinde!"

He wiped a hand on the back of his apron and thrust it
at me.

"Simon Fernandez. May I just say that your remarks at your
father's funeral were very moving."

"That's very kind of you."

"Not at all, not at all. Only I didn't think it appropriate to tell
you at the time."

He gave a slight nod to Bee, and she stuck her hand out as
well.

"Beth Raven, a childhood friend of the pastor."

"I'm pleased to meet you, Miss. Raven. Would the two of
you join me in my workshop?"

He led us through the door at the back of his shop. The
workshop was small, but efficiently organized. One wall was
covered with hooks, each at the top of an outline of the tool
which belonged there. All the tools but two hung in their
proper place. The ones that didn't—a chisel and a hammer—
were on the small workbench, bathed in the light from a
skylight, next to a carving in process. Everything in the room
was spotless and cared for.

I took the opportunity to verify the impression that had
occurred to me outside the shop.

"I think you made a box that my father owned. Beautifully carved, with a frog statue to sit on the top?"

"Yes, indeed. The lily pond. It was your father's inspiration. I can take a bit of credit for the final design, and of course the actual carving. We were young men, then."

"Did you create his walking stick as well?"

The question seemed to make him nervous.

"I don't work in stone."

I decided it was time to get down to business.

"We won't take up much of your time, Mr. Fernandez, but Henry told us that you might be able—"

"Henry? Henry who?"

I was surprised that I couldn't answer that.

"I don't actually know his last name. He works at the Thirsty—"

But he was shaking his head decisively.

"I'm afraid I don't know anyone by that name. But I do think I may have your father's original sketches for that box you spoke of. Come on back and I'll look through the files."

And with that he took my Bible out of my hand and placed it on the workbench, giving me a look that clearly meant something, though I didn't know what.

He led us through another door, down a short hallway, and into a much larger workroom with multiple workbenches and shelves—all crammed with clockwork, as near as I could tell.

Some of the actual clocks were easy to spot because they resembled the only one I had ever seen, at the Thirsty Angel.

Others seemed to be toys of one kind or another. He showed us figures that walked toward the edge of a table, powered by a weight hanging over the edge. There was a wooden box with a lever on the top. If you pushed the lever, a lid opened and a carved wooden hand came out to push it back. There were elaborate structures of wheels and strings and moving balls, and a small box that played a tune. Still others I could make no sense of at all.

He allowed himself a small smile of pride at our expressions.

"I'm sorry about my behavior in the store, but when you're in my profession you have to be very careful about what conversations might be overheard. It should be quite safe to talk here—or if it isn't," he smiled, "I have bigger problems than our conversation."

"Why did you leave my Bible out there?"

"I was probably being overly cautious. There are those who think it's possible to eavesdrop through a Bible. I doubt it, but better safe than . . ."

"It's just that my father thought the same thing," I said. "Toward the end."

"Did he? Well, that makes me doubt it less. So my friend Henry sent you?"

"Yes. We need to find a sorcerer, rather quickly. He thought that perhaps you could . . ."

He peered thoughtfully at us over his glasses while we explained our problem. When we had finished explaining about Lucky and the unofficial police rod, he frowned and nodded.

"Well," he said, "I have good news and bad for you. I can certainly connect you to a sorcerer—and she will talk to you if I vouch for you. That's the good news."

"She?"

"Yes. This sorcerer is a woman."

"And the bad news?"

"The bad news is that she is a good person."

"I'm sorry . . . ?"

"I doubt very much that she would have any dealings with the chief of police, and I also doubt that she would create a device for killing. So she's probably not the sorcerer you are looking for."

"I see."

"We'd like to talk to her anyway," Bee said. "She might be able to tell us something useful."

"Of course. I'll give you her address. You will say that a Mr. Sullivan told you about her art collection, and that you would like to see it."

Just before we left I had another thought.

"Mr. Fernandez, do you *repair* clockwork as well?"

"You have clockwork you want repaired?"

I told him about the secret compartment in my office.

He chuckled.

"A pastor who wishes to talk to a sorcerer and uses clockwork to conceal a secret bookcase. You are going to cause me to revise my expectations of the clergy. I'll see you after the service on Sunday to schedule an appointment for 'spiritual counseling' sometime next week. You'll have me come to the parsonage, and meet with me in your office."

"You must do this sort of thing a lot."

He shook his head.

"Not often, but that is how your predecessor and I arranged things when I installed that panel for him."

THE THIRSTY ANGEL was a different experience in the daytime. It was partly a change in the moods and energy of the customers, but it was also a matter of light. There were windows up high near the ceiling in three of the walls, and daylight streamed through them, giving a golden glow to the walls, the clock, the wooden floor—even to the waiters as they hurried from kitchen to tables and back again.

Henry—who seemed to be as much of a fixture as the

owner—saw us to our table and took our drink orders. I took the opportunity to satisfy my curiosity.

"You're not the only one who draws conclusions, Henry."

He stopped and considered that.

"I've drawn another just now, sir."

"And what's that?"

"That you are about to share one of your own with me."

I laughed.

"Would I be right in thinking that Gabriel Hauser was not the original owner of this establishment?"

"And what would make you think that?"

"The name of the place. Mr. Hauser despises anything supernatural, whether it's related to the church or to sorcery. So he would be very unlikely to name a business he started himself after something as supernatural as an angel."

Henry chuckled.

"I can tell you from experience, sir, that drawing conclusions is a risky business."

"Then I'm wrong?"

"Mr. Hauser is the only owner this business ever had, and he named it himself."

"How remarkable."

"There is an explanation."

But we were interrupted.

"Pastor Kinde?"

Henry paused and looked up at the couple standing next to my seat.

Everything about them screamed "holder", from the clothes they wore to the way they stood to the air of entitlement in their smiles. The fact that his forehead and hands were bare of any logo merely confirmed the obvious.

Except that she was the one who had spoken to me, while he remained silent.

I stood.

"How can I help you?"

She smiled.

"I'm Rose. May we join you?"

It turned out that the single dish on the lunch menu was a bacon, lettuce, and tomato sandwich. Plates for lunch, bowls for supper. While they ordered I got a closer look at Rose. She wore the same monkish gloves that Beth had worn that Thursday at the Humble Monk—which seemed like a lifetime ago—and she showed no sign of removing them. Her hair was cut with bangs, which completely covered her forehead. There was no way to tell if she was wearing a logo or not.

After we had all ordered, Rose's companion finally addressed us.

"Before we get to anything else, we all need to be clear that this conversation is confidential. You will be free to use whatever you learn here, but under no circumstances are you to tell anyone where you learned it, or to involve Rose in any way. If you can't agree to that, then we will be on our way."

"And what," Bee said, "makes you think you can trust us to keep our word?"

"Rose has a great deal of faith—perhaps too much—in Kate Ford's impression of you. I, on the other hand, have researched the pastor thoroughly. He has a reputation for keeping his word."

"And what about me?" she asked.

He locked eyes with her for a moment without speaking. Some understanding passed between them.

"I don't expect you would be any less trustworthy than the pastor."

Bee merely nodded. He continued.

"So are we all in agreement?"

Bee said, "We are."

"Pastor?"

"Yes," I said.

"Good. Rose?"

Rose smiled and patted his hand.

"Thank you, darling."

She turned her attention to us.

"You want to know about Lucy, right? I guess you already know she was one of the women Tho recruited to entertain his 'important friends.' I was, too, only I got recruited a bit before her. Tho got her by threatening her water rations; he got me by supplying medicine for my ailing mother—then threatening to withhold it if I didn't do as he said.

"Lucy wasn't as fast a learner as I was, and she didn't have my advantages. I had relatives in the village as a child, and grew up with more of what Tho called 'polish.' I realized quickly that there was no percentage in fighting Tho, and that the sensible thing would be to learn as much as I could about the world of holders while I figured out how to escape him—and to make friends if I found anyone worthy. I actually found several worthy. His guests weren't all as corrupt as he assumed."

She smiled at her companion.

"But Lucy . . . Lucy got to be a sort of favorite of one of them —a holder named Matt Anwir—oh, you know him?"

I nodded.

"I've met him through Boyd Franklyn," I said. "He struck me as . . . dangerous."

"Very. And cruel as well. I can't imagine what he put Lucy through. But he had one weakness. He didn't believe that anybody below his own social status really existed. So he tended to talk in front of his servants, and in front of Lucy, as though they were part of the furniture.

"He had been buying black-market water from Tho for some time, and he had Tho involved in a larger plot to do Boyd Franklyn out of his water rights entirely. Lucy thought she could use that information to be rid of Tho.

"I told her there was only one way to do that—to go

straight to Boyd Franklyn and tell him everything. She didn't want to. She was too ashamed of what Tho had made her do. She thought she could simply use the information to blackmail him into letting her go. I guess you know how that turned out."

Her eyes misted.

"Is there anything else you want to know?"

Bee reached out to her.

"Do you need any help?"

"That's very kind. I don't, actually. My mother died, so Tho can't use her against me anymore. And Hugh is very skillful at dealing with people like Tho."

She put her hand on his.

"I'll be moving to his estate. It's on the East Coast."

Hugh put his other hand on top of hers.

"You see," he said, "we wouldn't want any of this rather sordid mess to follow Rose to her new life."

They left without touching their sandwiches.

Bee and I munched on ours in silence, digesting what we had just heard. Eventually, she spoke up.

"We need to warn Boyd."

I nodded.

"Though he may already know. I'm still trying to figure out how any of this helps Lucky."

"Well, it certainly injures Tho's credibility, but unless there's another connection . . ."

"Exactly. And his hearing is tomorrow afternoon."

Henry showed up with fresh beers.

"Your guests didn't finish their lunch."

"No, Henry. I don't think they were all that hungry."

"Probably used to a higher quality of food."

"I'm not sure that's possible, Henry. The food here is not fancy, but it's very good."

"I thought I might enlighten you a bit further."

"Oh. About the name of this restaurant? You said there was an explanation?"

"I did. And the explanation is a name, as well. But that's not what I meant just now. It's only just occurred to me about your friend's friend—Will Terren—that you may not know where he lived."

"No one knows."

"Would that be a conclusion of yours, sir?"

I laughed.

"*You* know?"

"I'm not the only one. The police know, as well."

I shook my head.

"Not unless they found out very recently."

"Will rented a room here, upstairs. And the chief has had it sealed up and left exactly as it was."

I turned to Bee.

"I don't think Dennis knows about this."

"It also occurred to me," Henry continued, "that if a couple of people wanted to be shown the room—unofficially, of course—that they might just show up at the back door around eight tonight."

"Thank you, Henry. They might just do that."

He smiled and turned to leave.

I grabbed his sleeve.

"Wait a minute. What about the name?"

"Oh, that. It's his own name that's the clue."

"Gabriel Hauser?"

"You've noticed how much he likes his beer."

Bee laughed out loud. I was still puzzled. She looked at me in disbelief.

"Gabriel!"

Henry nodded.

"The thirsty angel in question is the proprietor himself."

Chapter 22

"So," I said, "do you think Rose's friend is going to marry her?"

We were walking across town to the address the clockmaker had given us for the sorcerer. The temperature had dropped since lunch, and clouds had begun to gather. I could smell the possibility of rain in the air.

Bee seemed a bit irritated by my question.

"I don't know. They seem happy enough."

"But if he's only taking her home to be his—"

She stopped and turned to face me.

"'Judge not, lest ye be judged.' You *do* read your Bible, right?"

"We can't just throw morality out the window."

"You can't just reduce it to a set of rules, either, Adam."

"Why not?"

"Because life just isn't that simple. Sooner or later you'll run into an exception to your rules."

"So everyone just does whatever they want to do?"

"Would that be so bad, most of the time? I remember asking you what you wanted to do about those books. I didn't find your answer to be so evil."

"The point is, you can't count on our fallen nature."

"You really *don't* read your Bible, do you? What did Joshua say to the multitudes? 'You are the light of the world.' Does that sound like a fallen nature to you? If you can't trust the light of the world to make a moral judgment, then . . . I give up."

She stalked off ahead of me.

THE SORCERER'S HOUSE STOOD ON the oldest street in the village. It had three floors, steep roof-lines, and stood in the center of an unkept garden. Even the path from the gate to the front door was overgrown, and required us to push branches out of our faces as we passed.

We knocked, and waited. Eventually we heard footsteps inside, and the door opened.

She was, of course, a member of my congregation—though I had no idea what her name was. She was tall and rather thin, with a very straight nose which dominated a face that seemed perpetually amused. Her black hair was tied back in a bun.

"Can I help you?"

"We're friends of Mr. Sullivan," Bee said. "He was very impressed with your art collection."

She smiled.

"Mr. Sullivan is rather easy to impress. I hope you won't be disappointed. Come in."

The inside of the house was much tidier than the garden, but almost as crowded. The walls were covered with drawings and paintings of all sizes and subjects and styles. Every surface held a small sculpture or art object of some kind. But there was a sense of order about the place in spite of that.

She led us through to a small dining room.

"I'm Isabelle Jordan, Pastor. And your companion?"

"I'm Beth Raven, an old friend."

"Would you like some tea?"

I spoke before Bee could accept.

"I'm afraid we don't have a lot of time."

"I see. Then let me give you the tour straight away."

She didn't move, but looked pointedly at my Bible. Bee nudged me, and I got the message. I put it on the table, and she led us out of the room.

"Normally," she said as we moved down the hall, "I would start with some of the lesser works. But as you're in a hurry I think we'll go straight to the gem of my little collection."

She opened a door at the end of the hall and motioned us into a tiny room, which held a single painting on the opposite wall.

"Let me get the lighting just right for you."

She closed the door behind us, and adjusted the light.

It was an odd painting, and obviously very old. If someone had described it to me I don't think I would have been impressed. It depicted a small bedroom, containing a single bed, a couple of chairs and a small table. There were some paintings hanging on the walls, and a window at the end of the room. The table held a pitcher and a bowl and some other objects.

It lacked the sense of reality my father put into his drawings, the style seemed almost amateurish in a way, and yet I don't think I would have ever tired of it.

I turned to see Bee's reaction, but at that moment the whole room shook.

Our hostess put a hand on each of our backs.

"Don't worry. We're quite safe."

I wasn't too alarmed. Growing up in the San Fernando Valley, I had plenty of experience with earthquakes, and this didn't feel like a serious one. Still, I was glad a moment later when the shaking stopped, and Isabelle opened the door.

"Now we can talk."

The hallway was gone.

In its place was a large well-lit room, about four times as wide as the hallway had been, and perhaps a little longer. The walls on either side had niches built in, some empty, some containing various objects: an ornate necklace, a black cube about six inches high, a statue of a very fat man wearing a robe, a translucent purple sphere which floated an inch or two above its shelf, a worn deck of playing cards.

The center of the room held a desk. It had clearly begun its life as a work of art—beautifully designed and crafted. But it had been well used, and obviously still was; its surface was cluttered with the same kinds of mementos and tools that covered my father's desk in his working days—even including a sketchpad and a selection of pencils.

Against the wall at the far end stood a large round table, its surface a dull black liquid. It was topped by an equally large transparent dome.

I pointed.

"Is that what I think it is?"

"What do you think it is?"

"When I was in seminary I only got to take the most basic 'Mind of God' courses—never the ones with a practicum. But one day I was moving some scenery for a school play, and passed the doorway to the workroom, just as someone was coming out..."

She nodded.

"Then I'm right?" I said. "It's a creation chamber?"

"The technical term is 'firmament.' I couldn't say, before, but I *was* expecting you. I thought you might like to witness something."

She led us past the desk to the domed table and stood in the center of a five-pointed star etched into the floor. She gestured with one hand, and light began to glow at the center of its liquid surface.

As we watched, a small green bump emerged from the liquid at the point of light, and slowly grew both higher and wider. The bump had an irregular surface which I found familiar, though I couldn't place the pattern at first. But by the time its base stopped increasing in width, and began to decrease, I knew what I was looking at: an exact replica of the stone on the top of my father's walking stick.

The stone rose higher in the dome, as the stick grew beneath it, and when it was finally complete it stood, balanced perfectly in the center.

Isabelle gestured once again, then reached through the dome and removed the stick. She carried it to the wall on one side of the room and placed it in an empty niche.

"It's a custom, started by my father. When someone who has been both a friend and a patron dies, we choose one of the projects they commissioned, and create a duplicate to remember them by."

"So you made his walking stick."

"My father did, before he died and I inherited the family trade."

"But . . . the chamber—the 'firmament'—it can create *wood*?"

"The cane isn't wood. It's all monkstone."

"I thought monkstone was . . ."

"It's not a particular substance. It's the result of a particular *word*."

I nodded understanding.

She turned to Bee.

"A particular pattern, or design, you understand."

Bee also nodded, and Isabelle turned back to me.

"But you didn't come here to talk theology. You wanted to ask something?"

We told her about the murder, and Lucky, and our question about the non-regulation police rod.

"Simon, the woodcarver, told us that you were too good a person to have dealings with Tho, but we were hoping you might be able to point us in the right direction."

"Simon is too kind. Tho commissioned it."

"You mean you *did*—"

"No. Heavens, no. But I was the first sorcerer he tried. I don't know how he got my name. He spent an hour trying to explain to me what he wanted—something that looked like a police rod, but would kill. Odd, that."

"Odd?"

"I get requests for weapons of one sort or another very often. I never create them, understand, and I'm not entirely sure how these people even find me. But they almost always want something deadly that looks innocuous. Something they can carry, or leave lying around without suspicion. This was the only time I ever had a request for a weapon that actually looked like a weapon."

She chuckled.

"I intentionally misunderstood everything he said. I showed him around my art gallery, treating him to endless lectures on various paintings and babbling on about herbal remedies. I pressed him to stay for tea, and told him how lonely it was living alone. I'm fairly certain that he left thinking I was dotty. But he was definitely looking for someone who could create exactly what you're describing."

"Could you tell us who might have done it?"

"Possibly, but you say your friend's hearing is tomorrow afternoon?"

"That's right."

"Then I would suggest you focus your attention elsewhere. The names I could give you probably won't talk to you—certainly not if they think you came from me. And what do you expect to get from them? They certainly won't testify on your friend's behalf. You now know for certain that the rod belongs to Tho. I don't know how you're going to use that information, but I'm quite sure that finding the sorcerer who made the rod isn't going to get you any further. Besides, they are dangerous people to even know."

I had to try.

"Would *you* testify? That Tho was trying to commission a lethal police rod?"

"Do me a favor. Warn Lucky to be careful with that Bible."

Dennis was just ahead of me on our way down the stairs to Lucky's cell.

"Careful?"

"He's your man, and I'm inclined to agree that he's innocent, so I'll turn a blind eye to minor indiscretions. But if we'd known he was chosen, we'd never have allowed him to have it. Just tell him to be discreet if he's conversing with you."

"He's not chosen."

"Are you sure?"

"What's this about?"

"I've been taking a personal interest, on your behalf. Bringing his food down myself, chatting with him to keep his spirits up, little things. This morning I heard him talking to someone as I approached his cell. I couldn't hear what they were saying, but—"

I laughed.

"Thank you, Dennis, for taking care of Lucky, but there's no indiscretion to overlook. Lucky is definitely not chosen. His Bible won't allow him to pray a word with anyone. But he does talk to it—especially when he's alone in his room. He gets so involved with the stories that he talks back to them. I've sometimes thought he had a guest in his room at the parsonage when he was only watching a morality play."

"You're sure he's not chosen? Because I could have sworn..."

"If he were chosen, I would know. It's not really something you can hide."

Chapter 23

"Almost every holder owned land in some form, and with the land came rights, in many cases due to laws or agreements dating prior to the Short Domination. The land itself was of little use except for very limited farming, and it could even be a nuisance, since it often was populated by squatters. But the rights could be nearly priceless."

Dorothy Kenning, *The Short Domination: A Student Primer*

I IMMEDIATELY REGRETTED TELLING Lucky about my conversation with Dennis. He laughed, but he seemed deeply embarrassed and quickly changed the subject.

"What have you learned, Lad? About Tho?"

"You were right about the rod. He definitely commissioned it, but I'm afraid we can't prove it. The sorcerer who told us won't come forward, for obvious reasons."

"I didn't expect he would. What did you learn about the woman they executed?"

"That was a bit more productive, but we still don't have a witness. Tho was using her to entertain visiting holders—apparently making himself friends in high places. He's been coercing squatter women in various ways for that purpose. The holder he assigned her to is plotting with Tho to steal Boyd's water rights, and she found out. She tried to blackmail Tho into letting her go, and he got her executed instead."

"You need to tell Boyd about this, Lad. Right away. Did you find out which holder it was?"

"Matt Anwir. I've met him once or twice through Boyd."

"Matt Anwir! I'd forgotten that. I saw the two of them together—Anwir and Tho—one night at the Thirsty Angel."

"I thought police weren't allowed to eat there."

"They aren't, but Tho was in disguise—not that I think he fooled the owner. They were sitting at the other end of the room from Terren and me. I should have told you this before. After a while Anwir left, but Tho just ordered another beer. The thing is, when we left, he left too. Outside, I turned toward the parsonage, but Terren went the other way, and so did Tho. I can't swear he was following Terren. It might have just been a coincidence. But still . . ."

I MET Boyd in his library. The overcast sky provided very little natural light, so the room was dark except for the little corner where he worked.

He looked up as I came in and put his Bible down.

"How's Lucky holding up?"

"Odd that you should ask that. I can't figure him out. He seems to be taking the whole thing in stride—better than I would."

"I've put out a few feelers, seeing if I could call in a favor or two on his behalf, but it all seems to come down to the hearing."

"That's what I've come to talk about. Bee and I have uncovered some information that seems to argue in Lucky's favor, but I don't know how to make use of it."

"What kind of information?"

"The police rod Tho planted in his room—"

"You can prove that?"

"Not exactly. But it wasn't a regulation rod. It was produced by a sorcerer, and commissioned by Tho."

"And you can prove *that*?"

"To my satisfaction, yes. And I hope to yours, as well. We've talked to the first sorcerer he approached, who refused the commission. She assures us that the rod Tho 'found' in Lucky's room is exactly what he tried to get her to make."

"Her?"

"Yes. A woman. But she refuses to testify, for obvious reasons."

"We could compel her."

"And get her executed instead? For helping us?"

"She *is* a sorcerer. Is that all you've turned up?"

"The other thing has to do with your problems. Lucky seems to think it's connected, though I can't see how. There was a woman executed last week in the village. Lucy Ford."

"Selling her favors for water."

"That was the charge, but the truth appears to be that she was coerced by Tho, who has been providing 'entertainment' to visiting holders, for purposes of his own."

"And this has something to do with me?"

"One of those holders is Matt Anwir."

"Ah."

"Lucy Ford discovered that Anwir had enlisted Tho in a plot—"

"To rob me of my water rights."

"That was the real reason she was arrested and executed."

"What's Tho's role in this conspiracy?"

"I don't know. Only that he's involved."

"And you have a witness?"

"Not one who will testify. But I wouldn't make this up."

"Oh, I believe you. You remember when I asked whether you were dealing in contraband? There's a board meeting early next week. Last Wednesday I was approached by a board member—Presbyter Brine. He alerted me to a conspiracy among the board members to wrest control of the corporation and sell off my water rights. He offered to throw his votes my way and save the corporation if I could retrieve that 'contraband' from you and give it to him."

"It was books."

"You *had* them?"

"Not when you asked me. Brine approached me directly after you and I talked—threatened my career—and Tho also tried to get them from me, first through Dennis, and then he threatened me directly. I found them, later, after the break-in, but they vanished the night of the murder, before I could turn them over."

"So you don't have them now?"

"I don't."

He stared into the darkened room, thinking. There was even less light than when I had arrived. I realized it was almost time for me to get back for the evening service.

He shook his head.

"I'm sorry, Adam. I should be focusing on Lucky's problems and instead I'm worried about the board meeting."

"It might all be related. How is Brine on your board? We—clergy, I mean—we're not allowed to hold stock."

"He doesn't. But my father left half of the family stock to

me, and half in trust to my mother. Brine sits on the board as her trustee."

He shot me a rueful smile.

"I might have tried harder to get rid of that blasted Lazarus Stone if it hadn't been for that. She's obviously in pain, and she keeps begging me to help her die, but when she dies all that stock will be mine."

"So you're—"

"Paralyzed. I can't try to help her because I'm afraid of my own motives. So I just prolong her suffering."

FRIDAY SERVICES WERE ALWAYS the hardest for me. I'd already preached the same sermon six times, and it was an effort not to just go through the motions while thinking of other things. But that evening I had so much else on my mind that I struggled to keep my place. I may have even skipped some parts.

Bee was waiting when I got back to the parsonage. I changed, and we scrounged the kitchen for a quick meal. Just before eight we set off for the Thirsty Angel. It hadn't rained after all, and we could even see patches of stars where the clouds parted.

The back door to the restaurant was actually on one side, down an alley. We tried it, but it was latched from the inside. I was debating whether to risk knocking when it swung open, and Henry gestured us in with a finger to his lips.

He led us up a stairway in silence, then down a narrow hall. The wallpaper was faded, and the air had the faint scent of old carpet. He stopped before a door that had an official notice tacked to it and a strip of paper glued across the crack between the door and the frame.

He held up a finger for us to wait, applied a wet sponge to the paper for a moment, then carefully peeled it back from the frame. Then he opened the door, ushered us in, and closed the door behind him.

"How long will you need, do you think?"

I exchanged a glance with Bee.

"About half an hour?"

He nodded.

"Don't try to leave until I come for you. I'll be gluing the paper back before I go, in case anyone comes down the hall."

And he was gone.

We stood with our backs to the door and surveyed the room. It was small—perhaps twelve feet square—with the same faded wallpaper as the hallway, and the same faded carpet. A narrow iron bedframe, topped by a thin mattress and well-worn blankets, stood in the corner to our left. A cheap wooden table and chair took up the remaining space at the foot of the bed.

A full-length mirror, framed in dark scratched wood, hung on the wall directly opposite us. Next to it, by the table, a window looked out onto the alley. To our right a small dresser stood between two doorways. There were no pictures on the walls.

The bed, the table, the dresser top, and much of the floor were stacked with books.

I threaded my way between the stacks to try the two doors. One led to a toilet and sink. The mirror above the sink opened to a shallow metal cabinet, empty except for rust. A razor and bar of soap lay on the back of the sink. Two more stacks of books flanked the toilet.

Bee had opened the other door to reveal a small closet. It contained a few clothes on hangers, and nothing else. The pockets were empty. A ladder was built into the wall, leading to an access panel—probably to the attic.

The drawers in the dresser were mostly empty. One

contained a few more items of clothing. I lifted the mattress, but there was nothing beneath it.

We turned our attention to the books. I didn't remember every title I had found in my office, but none of the titles stacked in Terren's room rang a bell.

I turned to Bee.

"Any ideas?"

She shook her head.

"If we had the time to go through all these books, maybe. He was probably just a dealer in illegal books."

"Still, he thought there was something special about mine —or one of them, anyway. And so did a lot of other people."

We stood there at a loss, staring at the piles of books, while the minutes ticked away.

Then we heard footsteps coming up the hall. More than one person.

We froze.

They stopped just outside, and there was a sound of paper tearing.

Bee pulled me into the closet and closed the door. It was close in there, hardly room for the two of us. We huddled together, listening.

I'd heard the first voice somewhere before, but I couldn't place it at first.

"You might be right."

The second voice was Tho's.

"They have to be. They aren't in the pastor's house. I can guarantee that. And we know our friend doesn't have them because he still wants them. And whoever killed Terren would have turned them over to him by now."

"But when would he have brought them here? Before he was killed? Then why murder him?"

"He must have gotten them earlier, before the night I broke in. Then he went back for something else. The murderer—

whoever he is—didn't know about this place, so he followed him, thinking he was going for the books."

"But why kill him?"

"Maybe the victim saw him. Maybe he figured he didn't have a choice, maybe he just saw a chance to eliminate the competition."

It was hard to follow. There were too many 'he's and 'him's. But I did recognize the other voice. It was Matt Anwir.

"What if the pastor moved them? Hid them somewhere else?"

"If he did I'll have them before the hearing. He won't let his servant be executed. But I don't think he did. That means they have to be here. I've kept my side of the bargain."

"Don't worry. You'll get your shares if they're here. You'll be a holder. I wish he'd told us more—enough so we'd know what to look for. I'll go through the place with you, but in the end I'll bet we're going to have to get him to come himself. You're going to drop the charges on the servant, right? We don't need to create an enemy in the church."

"That's my business. The pastor needs to be taught a lesson."

Bee nudged me, then pointed to the ladder and the ceiling. I nodded, and she climbed swiftly and silently to the top. The panel made a slight pop as she lifted it, and for a moment I thought we were heard. But the door to the closet didn't open, so I followed.

Chapter 24

Squatter proverb

WE EMERGED IN A LOW-ROOFED ATTIC, full of dust and cobwebs. There was ozone in the air, and we could hear rain pounding on the roof above us. I slid the panel back into place as quietly as I could and we began to crawl from one rafter to the next, toward a dim light at the back of the building. It was murder on the knees, and once Bee exclaimed when she scratched her hand on the sharp end of a nail.

Eventually we reached the light, which proved to be an air vent in the back wall of the building. I wiggled it back and forth, working it slowly free, and then, just when I got it loose, I lost my grip. It dropped out of sight and hit below with a sort of dull thud. We sat back and waited for someone to investigate, but no one came.

We were two stories high. The back side of the building had no windows or drainpipes or anything to help us down. I considered trying to get up to the roof, and then to an easier exit, but decided there would be too much danger of slipping in the rain.

Directly below us was an open trash bin, which accounted for the quiet landing of the air vent. I had no idea whether it contained anything we would want to fall into.

It was the only option, though.

I took off my belt, looped one end around my hand and gripped it tightly. I had Bee do the same with the other end, then she eased her way backward through the vent hole until she dangled above the trash bin, closer by the length of my belt, my arm, and as much of my body as I dared let hang over the edge. She let go and dropped safely into the bin.

I was going to have to drop farther. I couldn't see any way to use the belt myself, so I let it drop, then worked my way back into the attic. I turned myself around and edged out feet first, until I was hanging by my fingertips.

It was a very long way down, and for a moment I considered trying to get back into the attic. But that wasn't a real possibility.

I let go.

Bee had cleared the bin of anything she thought looked dangerous before climbing out, and I fell safely. But I landed on my own leg, and it twisted under me.

I looked up to meet Bee's eyes, staring at me over the edge of the bin, and I giggled. Her face broke into a smile, and then we were both laughing and couldn't stop.

After a time we calmed down, and I tried to stand. A pain shot through my leg, and I collapsed back into the trash. It took us some time to get me out of the bin—because of my leg, because everything was soaked and slippery, but mostly because every setback started us laughing again.

Once I was out, I found I couldn't put any weight on my leg, so I put an arm around her shoulders, and we hobbled along, Bee acting as my crutch, all the way back to the parsonage.

WE STUMBLED through the front door, soaked to the skin. I grabbed the banister and Bee slipped out from under my arm.

"Wait here."

She dashed up the stairs, leaving me balanced on my good leg and dripping on the carpet. She was back in a moment, carrying my father's walking stick.

"This should help. Besides, I always thought it would look good on you. Do you think you can make it upstairs?"

"Upstairs?"

"We have to get you out of those wet things."

With the walking stick on one side and Bee on the other the stairs were manageable. I changed into dry clothes, then loaned Bee a pair of slacks and one of my shirts. When she had changed we worked our way back down the stairs.

When we reached the couch she slipped out from under my arm again and faced me. Her eyes drifted from mine to my lips.

"Sit. I'll make us some tea."

She turned to go.

"No," I said.

She turned back, a question in her eyes.

"Stay," I said.

I dropped the walking stick, and she stepped into my arms.

After a time, we sank to the couch.

Then we didn't talk for a very long time.

Eventually we did talk, but not about Lucky or Anna or theology.

And then we didn't talk again, but sat quietly together, my arm around her, the weight of her head on my chest, the scent of her hair, the pounding rain outside the window . . .

It was Bee who finally stirred and brought us back to the troubles of the day.

"This is very nice, but . . . Lucky."

I sighed, and prayed the light up.

"You're right, of course."

I moved my arm. She sat up a little straighter.

"So Tho was being offered the chance to be a holder."

"And they're both working for someone else."

I raised her hand to my lips. She smiled.

"When Tho talked about the murder, did it sound to you like—"

"Like he knew exactly what had happened?"

"That's what I thought."

I traced the Raven logo on the back of her hand with my finger. I stopped at the very edge, and looked closer.

She tensed.

"What's the matter, darling?"

"Nothing, probably. It's just . . . did you know Will Terren?"

She shook her head.

"You're sure?"

"Why would you think—"

"Sorry, but I have to ask this. If I were to scrub this logo with soap, would it come off?"

She pulled her hand back.

"That's a different question. And something we're going to have to talk about."

"You're a Human?"

"I would have told you, you know."

"And that means an infidel as well, right?"

"Well, that would depend on your definition—"

"This is a problem."

"It doesn't have to be."

"How could you have led me on like that?"

"It wasn't exactly a plan."

"I'm a pastor, Bee. I can't possibly . . ."

Her face crumbled, and for a moment I thought she was going to burst into tears. But she didn't. She straightened herself, hardened her expression, took a deep breath, and looked me in the eyes.

"If that's the way it is, I'll be very, *very* disappointed, darling. But right now we need to concentrate on helping Lucky."

"It's just that—"

"When that's over we can talk about this again."

I was afraid we never would, but I didn't want to argue about it either.

"Okay," I said. "So, about Lucky . . ."

My heart wasn't in it, and I didn't think hers was either. It took her a long time to respond—so long I thought I should probably just suggest we call it a night. But then her expression shifted, and a real question came into her eyes.

"Wait! Why did you ask if I knew Will Terren?"

"Because of your logo. It was blurred at the edge, the same way his was—before we scrubbed it off."

"Terren was a Human? But that means—Adam, I know why he had all those books!"

"Why?"

"He wasn't a dealer. He was an archivist!"

"I don't understand."

"He didn't want to steal the books, not permanently. He wanted to catalog them. We've got to go back there. Right now."

"Tonight?"

"I didn't know he was a Human before. I didn't know what to look for. We may have missed something really important."

She stood up and headed for the door.

I grabbed my walking stick and struggled to my feet.

"Bee! Wait!"

She stopped. I continued.

"We can't go tonight. I can hardly walk, there's no one to let us in, Tho might still be there—there's a thousand reasons. We'll go first thing in the morning, and take Dennis with us."

She looked down at my walking stick, then nodded.

"Of course. You're right. I'm too tired, anyway. We'll be fresher in the morning. I'll see you first thing."

She paused.

"Do you want me to help you upstairs?"

"I'm going to sit up for a while. I'll see you in the morning."

<hr>

AFTER A WHILE IT STOPPED RAINING.

I was still on the couch, my mind flitting from one place to another, from Lucky to Tho to Will Terren to Boyd to Anna, but always returning to Bee. How I had hurt her. How I loved her. How, against all my better judgment, I wanted more than anything to justify marrying her.

All our arguments made sense now. We belonged to two completely different worlds. But none of that mattered to me.

I kept revisiting the first time I'd seen her at the Humble Monk; the night she took over when my father died; the time she tried to steal the Lazarus Stone.

The Lazarus Stone.

I sat bolt upright.

I'd told her all the reasons we couldn't do that, and I'd even thought she'd agreed, but then she tried to steal it anyway.

I grabbed my walking stick and struggled to my feet, then out the door to my chariot.

I LEFT my chariot in front of the Thirsty Angel, then limped toward the alley that ran down the side. The street was wet and silent. The buildings were dark. The only light came from the statue of Joshua on the corner, and a sliver of moon that peeked through a break in the clouds.

There was more light when I rounded the corner of the alley, coming from one of the second-story windows. I leaned against the corner of the building for a second, resting my leg, and considered. I could be wrong, of course. She might have just gone home.

But I wasn't wrong.

A door slammed at the other end of the alley, and Bee came sprinting toward me, still dressed in my slacks and shirt, a look of grim determination on her face.

Before I could get my balance, the door opened again, and Tho stepped out. He aimed a police rod at her back and an arc of bright blue light knocked her off her feet.

I don't think he saw me, and he apparently had no question about what he had accomplished, because he didn't pause to see the outcome but disappeared back into the building.

She was only ten feet away, but it took me an eternity to reach her.

I hadn't brought my Bible, so I couldn't have prayed for help, but the healers appeared anyway. It took two of them to drag me away from her. They helped me lean against the wall, and one stayed with me while the other retrieved my stick.

A third knelt over Bee. It didn't take him long before the ambulance turned black and they took her body away.

Chapter 25

"We all experience our dark hours, and when we are in
them they can seem to deny even the possibility of light,
but the thing to do in those moments is to persevere, to
move on in search of the dawn."

Adam Kinde, *The Collected Sermons of Adam Kinde*

"Do you think you can listen to reason now?"

I was at Dennis' house, at his kitchen table. He was across
from me in a robe, his Bible by one elbow, a coffee mug by the
other, his hands clasped under his chin.

The wall behind him was yellow, and the aroma of fresh
coffee filled the room. A toy horse lay on its side near the door,
next to a couple of brightly colored blocks. Dennis' wife had
gone back to bed after making the coffee.

I had banged at his door in the middle of the night, and
burst into his house demanding that he arrest Tho immediately

for murder. It had taken him some time to even get me lucid, then more time to get the kind of details out of me that he could try to verify, and even more to get me halfway rational.

"Well?" he asked. "Can you?"

"I'm not going to let him get away with this, Dennis. If you won't do anything—"

"Did I *say* I wouldn't do anything?"

"He has to pay."

"Did I?"

My breath was ragged, like the rest of me.

"No," I conceded. "No. You didn't."

"I am going to do everything I can, Adam. Everything. And that's a lot more than you'll get without me. But we need to sort through this mess and figure out exactly what 'everything' is, and how to manage it."

"It's murder, Dennis. I was an eyewitness. How complicated can it be?"

He sighed.

"Very complicated, unfortunately. I'm going to take you through this again. And then I'll do it again, if necessary, and again—until you can see what we're up against and can manage to be a help instead of a hindrance."

He took a sip of his coffee.

"Okay?"

I nodded, reluctantly.

He pointed to my cup.

"Take another sip."

"Dennis, I'm not—"

"Take another sip."

I took another sip. It was hot and strong. He continued.

"Okay. Background. And pay attention to this. Point one: You want me to arrest my own boss. Given the nature of my boss, and the fact that I believe you, there's nothing I would rather do. But you can see the difficulty, right?

Unless we can figure a way to make this airtight—and get the proper authorities on our side before we act—I'll be the one who ends up in a cell. Can you get that through your head?"

"Okay. Yeah. But how are we going to—"

"Point two: You are a private citizen—clergy or not—accusing a police chief of murder. Can you guess which way the hearing will be biased? And, if you lose, can you guess what will happen to *you*?"

"I don't care what happens to me—I just want—"

"Fine. You don't care what happens to you. But what about your friends? When I've lost my job for supporting you, and you're in jail—or executed—for whatever crime Tho decides to pin on you, how are you going to help Lucky? How are you going to help Boyd?"

I hadn't thought much about Lucky or Boyd in the last few hours.

"Okay. Go on."

He took another sip.

"We are not in a strong position to begin with. So much for background. Now for your case. Point one on that: You are the only witness."

"How many witnesses do you need? I watched him do it."

"Even your scriptures require two, as I recall."

"Don't, Dennis."

"Okay. You're right. I'm sorry. But were you paying attention to my background points? You need an exceptionally strong case. And what you have, so far, is your word against his, and—point two—no body."

"That's got to be a mistake. I was there. I saw the healers. I saw them take her away."

"Just like you saw him kill her. But according to the healers no ambulance went out last night."

"You don't believe me."

"I *do* believe you. I'm just pointing out how the whole thing will look."

"So she's supposed to have vanished into thin air?"

"That's point three. And I want you to actually hear it this time around. He'll simply argue that she never existed."

"But you've met her!"

"Exactly. The officer arresting his own boss met her. The only witness to the crime met her. Lucky—a servant of that witness and a man facing his own charge of murder—met her. All three are suspect."

"What about Boyd? He not only met her, he knows her well."

"Boyd will help, but he isn't going to be enough. What about his mother?"

I shook my head.

"I can't drag her into this. Not in her condition."

"So who else met her? And how many of them knew her well enough to swear that the person they met was actually *Bee*?"

I thought of Kate the squatter, Rose, Henry, Simon the clockmaker, and Isabelle the sorcerer. Most of them wouldn't testify, and the rest wouldn't be believed. I felt the wind go out of my sails.

"No one."

"And even if Boyd is believed, that's only evidence that she *existed*, not that she was murdered or that she was even who she claimed to be. You know what I found when I researched her. She's not part of the Raven family, and even the owners of the house she 'rented' in town have never heard of her."

He leaned an inch closer.

"She was a Human—an infidel. They apparently retrieve their own dead. However they managed it, they got her body back and we may never be able to trace a thing about her."

I took another sip of coffee to give myself time to think.

"Okay," I said. "Okay. Maybe we can't get him for Bee's murder, but what about Will Terren's? You have *his* body."

"Will Terren?"

"There are some things you need to know."

I LIMPED through the front door of the parsonage around three in the morning, completely exhausted. I hadn't been able to convince Dennis to do anything about Tho anytime soon, Lucky's hearing was that afternoon, and Bee was dead.

Bee was dead.

And I would mourn her. I would. But first I had to avenge her, or at the very least save Lucky for her. Then I would mourn.

After.

I navigated the difficult trip up the stairs to my room, walking stick on one side and banister on the other, then collapsed onto my bed. I considered getting up again to undress, but my heart wasn't in it. I leaned my stick within reach, adjusted the pillow, and arranged my aching muscles into the least uncomfortable position. Just before I prayed the light out I saw her clothes, hanging on the back of a chair.

It came of itself, sobs wracking my body, snot pouring from my nose, tears blinding my eyes. It didn't stop, and it didn't occur to me to try to stop it. It just went on and on without pause or variation until there was nothing left.

Not even me.

THERE WAS a warm spot on my face. I brushed at it with one hand, but it didn't go away. I turned my head a bit and the warmth and light was on my eyelids.

Morning.

I stretched, and was surprised that the ache was mostly gone from my muscles. Then I opened my eyes and saw Bee's clothes, still hanging on the chair. I watched them awhile, mindless and sad, then heaved myself upright. My leg seemed much better.

I reached for my Bible and prayed the time.

It was already eleven.

The hearing was at one.

I prayed a word with Boyd, and convinced him to drop everything to meet me at the Humble Monk. Then I shaved and showered and dressed in record time.

I could have gotten to the Monk without my walking stick, but I carried it anyway.

She had liked it.

I didn't expect to be hungry, but discovered I was starving. I ordered breakfast, and had eaten most of it by the time Boyd arrived.

The first thing I had to do was break the news about Bee. That wasn't easy, and it naturally moved us into the other matters, because his first instinct was to ask for a postponement of Lucky's hearing, based on her death.

I had to convince him of what Dennis had finally gotten through my thick head the night before—that as far as anyone but us knew she hadn't died, had never even existed. It was almost noon before we got around to talking strategy.

It took another half hour to fill him in on everything else— what we had overheard in Will Terren's room, Tho's role in the plot against him, the origin of the murder weapon, all of it.

By the time I finished, he was as discouraged as I was.

"I'm afraid," he said, "that your detective friend is right."

He traced the pattern in the tablecloth with his finger.

"You're right too, of course. It all points to Tho. The problem is, you can't prove enough of it to move the charge to him from

Lucky. Tho almost certainly had the weapon, but your one witness won't come forward. He also had a strong reason: to retrieve these books and become a holder. But Bee—the only one who heard that besides you—is dead."

He paused at that, and took a moment to gain his voice back.

"I wish we didn't have to deal with this today. It seems so . . . Anyway, where was I? We can't prove he had the weapon, we can't prove he had a reason, and I don't see how we can even prove he was there."

"That," I said, "is the one thing we may be able to prove."

He looked up at me.

"How?"

"We have to get Lucky permission to consult the Book of Deeds. Lucky was there. We know that. So it's not only a way to clear Lucky, it just might implicate Tho as well."

He spread his hands and shook his head.

"I've done everything I can about that. Believe me. And I've been blocked at every turn."

<hr>

"I CAN'T GIVE you much time," Dennis said. "I have to have him in the hearing room and ready in fifteen minutes."

He left Lucky and me together, closing the door to the cell behind him.

"Well?" Lucky said.

"There's more to say than we have time for, so I'm just going to tell you the bare minimum. We know, but can't prove, that Tho had the weapon made, and that he had strong reasons to be there that night. So far, though, we can't prove he *was* there. I'd hoped to get you a reading, and that it would show him or something that pointed to him—or at least would clear you but Boyd doesn't think that's possible."

Lucky was thoughtful.

"If Tho did it, we need a reading for *him*."

"He's not going to give us one."

"Unless you figure out how to make him."

"There's something else. Bee's dead."

"Bee?"

His jaw dropped and a tear formed at the corner of his eye.

"Bee," he repeated.

I steeled myself, and continued.

"Tho killed her. I saw it myself. But there's no way to prove that either."

He pulled his attention back to me.

"Tho?"

"Yes. So we have to—"

A fierce look entered his eyes.

"No. Listen to me, Lad. You have to get Tho to agree to a reading. No matter what else happens. Understand?"

"He's just not going to, Lucky. Would you, if you were him?"

Dennis opened the door.

"It's time, Lucky."

He took him by the arm and led him out of the cell.

Lucky turned to look at me as they went down the hall.

"Get him to agree, Lad. Find a way."

Chapter 26

Dorothy Kenning, *The Short Domination: A Student Primer*

I HAD no experience of official hearings. The closest I had ever come had been an ecclesiastical inquiry into the death of a student at the seminary when I was seventeen. Because it was entirely a church matter, there had been no danger of an execution.

This hearing was quite different. Lucky could be dead before the end of the day.

The inquiry at the seminary had been held in the chapel—a large open space, with high ceilings and stone arches—and the entire school had attended, literally hundreds of students and faculty. The hearing room at the police station was claustrophobic by comparison. It was small and squarish, with an eight-foot ceiling, no windows, and only two doors: one directly behind the tribunal's desk, which was on a slightly raised platform at the front and center of the room, the other at the back wall, where I entered.

The executioner—the same man who had killed Lucy Ford just a little over a week before—sat at a smaller desk to the left of the platform. Lucky was seated a few feet away in a chair against the left wall, flanked by two officers.

The reader's desk, which was vacant, was to the right of the platform, and Tho was seated a few feet from that, in a larger and more comfortable chair than Lucky's, against the right wall, facing Lucky. A chair for witnesses was positioned a few feet in front of Lucky's, facing Tho, so that the tribunal and the rest of the room could see the face of each witness as they testified. Lucky would only be able to see the back of each witness' head—presumably to keep him from making eye contact.

A short wooden railing separated all this from the rest of us. There were only two rows of benches on our side of the railing, filled with what I supposed were witnesses. Gabriel Hauser and Henry from the Thirsty Angel were there, as was Dennis. I didn't know most of the rest.

When everyone had settled, the door at the front opened, and the tribunal entered. He was a tall thin man with slanted eyes and thin hair, combed straight back. He didn't look like he'd had a happy day in his life. He took his seat, perused his Bible for a moment, then banged his gavel and addressed the room.

"I'm Judge Michael O'Hara. Judge Ito is sick today, so I'll be running this hearing. We are here to determine who murdered Will Terren last Sunday evening, and to sentence that individual once his guilt is proved to my satisfaction. The police have produced only one suspect for our investigation: Das Baethan, the prisoner before us."

He turned to Lucky.

"Mr. Baethan, how would you like us to address you during this proceeding?"

Lucky took a moment to decipher that.

"Address me? Oh. Most people just call me Lucky."

Tho chuckled at that. The tribunal gave him a withering glance.

"I would remind you, Chief Tho, that while the irony is not lost on me, I will not tolerate insensitivity in this hearing. This man's life is on the line. It's not a time for levity."

He turned his attention back to Lucky.

"Very well, Lucky. You are accused of killing Will Terren last Sunday evening. Did you?"

"No, sir. I didn't."

He made a note in his Bible.

"The accused denies the charge. In that case, Lucky, we'll all be here for a while. Do you wish to designate someone in this room as your questioner?"

"My questioner?"

"Someone who may ask questions of the witnesses during the hearing, to make sure your side of the story is fully represented."

"Pastor Kinde."

The tribunal glanced at me.

"And you accept this duty, Pastor Kinde?"

"I do."

"Chief Tho will conduct the investigation. If at any time you wish to question one of his witnesses, simply raise your hand and I'll give you the opportunity."

He nodded to Tho, who stood and took a step forward.

"Detective Troy, please take the chair."

Dennis went through the little gate in the center of the railing and sat in the witness chair. One of the officers sitting next to Lucky rose, and took a book from the tribunal's desk—

much like the ones in Boyd's library, but bound in what I guessed was black leather. The pages, or at least their edges, were a sort of tarnished gold color. He held it out, and Dennis put his hand on it. I realized it must be an antique paper Bible.

"Do you swear," the officer said, "to tell no lies, and to omit nothing from your testimony which is of importance to this investigation, at the peril of your soul?"

"I do."

He replaced the Bible, and Tho stood facing Dennis.

"You were present during the accused's questioning after his arrest, Detective Troy?"

"I was."

"And what was the story which he told at that time?"

"He said he had come into the hallway just in time to see the victim leaving the pastor's office. That the victim had fled down the stairs, and that by the time he—the accused—had reached the top of the stairs, the victim was lying dead at the bottom."

"Did you have any doubts about this story at all?"

Dennis sent a nervous glance my way before answering.

"Well, I did wonder why it took him so long to get to the top of the stairs. The hall isn't that long, and he was pursuing someone who he thought shouldn't be there."

"So you didn't think his story made sense?"

"It bothered me a little."

"And did he say whether he had seen the victim before?"

"No. That is, he said that he had not seen the victim before."

"And was he lying about that, as well?"

The tribunal interrupted.

"Be careful, Chief Tho. I don't hold with questioners twisting the words of witnesses. The detective has not testified that the accused lied about his movements at the time of the murder. He has only testified that he had some doubts."

"Sorry, sir." He turned back to Dennis. "Was Lucky lying when he said he didn't know Will Terren?"

"Yes. We found witnesses who saw him and Terren drinking together more than once."

Tho looked my way.

"Any questions, Pastor?"

I shook my head.

Tho then called a whole series of witnesses from the Thirsty Angel: Gabriel, Henry, and a long list of regulars. Each of them said the same thing. Lucky and Will Terren had met regularly there for weeks prior to the murder.

I thought it was overkill. Dennis' testimony had already made the point. Then I realized what Tho was up to. He wasn't driving home the point that Lucky knew Will. He was driving home the point that Lucky had lied, and by implication that the rest of his testimony couldn't be trusted.

By the time he finished we had been there almost two hours, and the tribunal called a brief recess.

I stepped outside for some fresh air, and Dennis followed me.

"Adam, I'm sorry about that. But I couldn't lie under oath."

"You told the truth. It was Tho who tried to twist it. Do you think the tribunal sees through him?"

"Maybe. We're fortunate that it isn't the regular judge. He's practically Tho's puppet. This guy seems to be his own man, at least."

When the hearing reconvened I lifted my stick to catch the tribunal's eye.

"Yes, Pastor?"

"I have some questions I would like to ask Lucky. Is that allowed?"

"It is in my hearings. Go ahead."

One of the officers took Lucky by the arm, guided him to the witness chair, and swore him in. I made my way through the little gate, and stood a few feet away from him, leaning on my stick with both hands.

"Let's start from scratch, Lucky. Did you lie about knowing Will Terren?"

"Yes. I did."

"And why did you lie about that?"

"I don't really know. I just panicked. It was stupid."

"And did you lie about anything else when you were questioned?"

He gave me a slightly suspicious look.

"What do you mean?"

"Sorry. Did you lie about seeing the victim at the end of the hall, or what you saw when you reached the top of the stairs?"

"Oh. No. I told the truth about that."

"Good. How did you come to know Will Terren?"

"He met me one day in town. He said we could help each other, offered to buy me a beer while he explained."

"And what did he want?"

"He thought you had some books. He thought I could tell him about them. I told him I'd never seen you with a book, but he didn't give up."

"Why did you keep meeting with him?"

"I wanted to find out what he was up to. I didn't trust him."

"What did you think he was going to do?"

"I don't know, but I wanted to protect you if I could."

"Thank you, Lucky."

I returned to my bench and Lucky started to get up, but Tho stopped him.

"Just a moment, Lucky. I have a question for you as well. You admit to lying about Will Terren?"

"I already said that."

"And the reason you give for that is that you panicked?"

"That's right."

"So what had you done wrong?"

"Sorry?"

"In my experience, when a witness panics, it's because he's hiding something—something he's done that he shouldn't have. But you've just spun us a tale of absolute innocence. What was the sin that you were so afraid we would discover?"

He was standing over Lucky, uncomfortably close. Lucky said nothing, and Tho didn't move.

Finally Lucky spoke.

"It wasn't you."

"What wasn't me?"

"The police, I mean. I wasn't afraid *you* would find out. It was the pastor. I hadn't told him about meeting Will, you see, and I should have."

Tho didn't move immediately. He seemed lost in thought. After a moment or two of silence, he surveyed the room and spoke.

"Officer Nestor, please take the chair."

Nestor turned out to be the police officer who had tested the rod Tho claimed to have found in Lucky's room. He confirmed that it was not a regulation police rod, that it was—unlike the regulation rods—capable of killing a human being, and that it appeared to be the work of a sorcerer.

Tho then called Randy Stevens, a small round-faced man with a perpetual smile. He strode to the front and through the gate as though he had been invited to a party, and stuck a hand out to Tho as he passed him.

When Tho ignored the proffered hand, it didn't appear to faze Randy at all, who was still beaming as he settled himself into the witness chair. When he'd been sworn in, he leaned back and raised his eyebrows, inviting Tho's first question.

"Mr. Stevens, have you ever seen the accused before?"

"Oh, yes. Many times. He was a regular at the Thirsty, him and the dead fella. They spent many an evening chatting over their beers."

"And has he ever spoken to you?"

"Well, that's what I'm here for, isn't it? Yeah, we spoke, one evening a couple of weeks ago. He came to me to ask about a sorcerer."

"What did he want to know?"

"Where to find one, of course. You see, everyone at the Thirsty knows I used to work for Old Jensen, before he was executed for plying his trade. Not that I had any truck with sorcery, myself. I just swept up around the place and did odd jobs. But Jensen was the real thing, all right. Everyone knows that. So he didn't get more than he deserved."

"And what did Lucky want from you?"

"He asked if I knew how to get in touch with a sorcerer. I get asked that a lot, even though Jensen's dead, and he's the only sorcerer I ever knew. People seem to think I know all the sorcerers around."

"Did he say why he wanted a sorcerer?"

"He didn't say, but of course he wanted something done, or something made, or such. Stands to reason, doesn't it? Why else does anyone go to a sorcerer?"

"Thank you, Mr. Stevens. Officer Bless, please take the chair."

Stevens rose and hesitated, then he addressed Tho.

"That'll be all, then?"

Tho looked at him as though he were out of his mind.

"Yes. Go."

Stevens gave Tho a quick wink, then hurried through the gate.

The tribunal interrupted.

"You'll need to stay until the end of the hearing, Mr. Stevens."

"Oh. Yes. I knew that. I just meant . . ."

He made his way to his seat, and was replaced by one of the officers who had been with Tho when he arrested Lucky. That officer testified that he had been in Lucky's room when they found the fake police rod. I raised my stick and asked whether he had seen the rod before the chief found it. He admitted he hadn't.

Tho then questioned the other officer who had been there that day, who told the same story. I asked the same question and got the same answer.

"And that wasn't the first time you searched my house," I said, "was it, Officer?"

"No, sir."

"You were one of the officers who searched it the Friday before, for these mysterious books."

"I was."

"And was I, or anyone else, warned of this search in advance?"

"No, sir."

"Tell me, Officer. What happens if you're doing a search for one thing, but turn up something different—something that's obviously illegal—in the process. Would you report that, or just ignore it?"

"Report it."

"And it's illegal for anyone but a policeman to own a police rod—whether it's regulation or not?"

"Yes, sir."

"Was a police rod turned up during that search?"

"Not to my knowledge, sir."

"And Lucky's room was searched that day?"

"Yes."

"So it would be a safe assumption that the rod wasn't there five days before Lucky was arrested?"

"I couldn't say, sir."

I addressed the tribunal.

"I would very much like to ask Mr. Stevens a few more questions, your honor."

"You should have done that when he was in the chair, Pastor. Nevertheless. Mr. Stevens, please take the chair again. You are still under oath."

Stevens was delighted to take the chair again.

"Mr. Stevens," I said, "when you were working for Old Jensen, did anyone ever ask him to create a weapon?"

"Quite a few. Probably even more. I didn't see everything he did, or know all of his clients—that's what he called 'em, 'clients'—but I knew of several—just from being around, sweeping and odd jobs—several who wanted weapons."

"Are any of those clients in this room?"

He got a very serious look on his face and made a great show of carefully surveying the entire room. He even studied the executioner and the tribunal, though I noticed he didn't look at Tho.

"I don't see anyone I recognize—from those days, I mean."

"And did you see any of the weapons he made?"

He beamed again.

"Oh yes, they would be lying right out in the open there, waiting to be picked up, until the client came. I'd walk right by them. Close enough to reach out and touch. Course I wasn't allowed to handle them—any of them, not just the weapons. Though especially the weapons, since they were so dangerous."

"And what did these weapons look like?"

"Now that's an interesting point. You'd expect them to look like weapons, wouldn't you? Well they didn't. Not one of 'em. They all looked like something else. Something natural. Something that fit the client, you see, and wouldn't draw notice. If you'd commissioned a weapon, Pastor, it might look like a Bible, or like your reversed collar, or that stick you carry. If his honor there commissioned one, it might look like a gavel. You see what I mean?"

"I do, Mr. Stevens. That's very interesting. So tell me, why would a sorcerer create a weapon that looked like, say, a police rod?"

He screwed his face into a shape intended to convey deep thought.

"A police rod. Well, that is a puzzle, Pastor. I don't know— unless! Unless he was making it for someone who normally carried a . . ."

He stopped himself, and his eyes flicked toward Tho. There was fear in them.

"I couldn't say, Pastor. I just can't imagine."

Tho asked Lucky to take the chair again after that. The tribunal was irritated, but said nothing.

"Lucky, I get the feeling that you are very loyal to Pastor Kinde."

"His family has been very good to me. I've known him since he was small."

"And if you thought he was in any danger, you'd naturally want to protect him?"

"I would."

"Did you perceive Will Terren to pose a danger to Pastor Kinde?"

"I thought he might."

"How far would you go to protect Pastor Kinde?"

"As far as was needed."

"Would you kill?"

"That wasn't needed."

"That's not what I asked. Would you kill if it were necessary to protect Adam Kinde?"

"I don't know. I hope I would."

A hint of triumph appeared in Tho's eye.

"You hope you would *kill*?"

"If I *had* to, to protect the Pastor. Yes. But I didn't."

"And, just for the record, you don't deny that you were in the house at the time of the murder?"

"I was there."

"Thank you."

I raised my stick. The tribunal nodded. I didn't bother to stand.

"Lucky, did you have a police rod of any kind on the day of the murder?"

"I did not."

"And could you see Will Terren at the time of the murder?"

"No. I hadn't reached the top of the stairs."

"And can you swear that there was no one else in the house at the time of the murder?"

"I can't. There may have been. There had to be."

"Thank you."

Tho addressed the tribunal.

"I have no more questions or witnesses, your honor."

"Do you have a final statement?"

"Only if the pastor does. Otherwise, I think the evidence speaks for itself."

"Pastor?"

"I would like to question one more witness."

The tribunal sighed.

"Very well. I see that it's already four thirty. We'll adjourn for an early dinner, and meet back here at quarter after five. I want to finish this hearing today."

Chapter 27

Boyd Franklyn, holder

"So how's it going in there?"

Boyd had been standing not far from the front door when we filed out. He signaled to me, and we walked to the Humble Monk together.

Neither of us was hungry, but I forced myself to order a kale salad because I wanted to be fortified for the rest of the hearing.

I shook my head.

"I have no idea. But it's almost over. Lucky's the only suspect —or at least the only one Tho's telling the hearing about. He lied about knowing Will Terren at first, and Tho's made a big thing out of that. Brought in a legion of witnesses. None of them testified to much important, but the cumulative impression was overwhelming. I've been appointed Lucky's questioner —which isn't a great help, since I didn't even know there was such a thing until they made me one. I'm sure, as local holder, you could wangle your way in."

"I shouldn't even be here now. There's nothing more I can do for Lucky at this point, but I still feel responsible. Guilty. It's all I've been able to think about all day, when I should be trying to avoid the coming disaster at the board meeting, or at the very least finding a way to help my mother."

"Anna's worse?"

"She's suffering terribly. She doesn't even try to hide it anymore. But that damn Lazarus Stone . . ."

I nodded. It was my turn to feel helpless and guilty. I realized I hadn't given Anna a thought since Lucky was arrested.

"I half promised her to do something, but I'm in the same position with your mother that you are with Lucky. I can't really do anything, and yet I feel responsible."

My salad came and I ate it quickly and in silence. Neither of us had anything more to say.

We walked back to the station together. Just before we got there, I put a hand on his shoulder.

"Give Anna my best, will you? And tell her I'm sorry I haven't been able to find a way."

"I will. Tell Lucky the same for me."

"Of course. It's not a completely lost cause yet, you know. Judge O'Hara seems to have an open mind, as near as I can tell."

Boyd froze. Then he grabbed my arm and pulled me away from the door.

"Judge O'Hara?" he said. "Not Ito?"

"You wish to question another witness, Pastor?"

"I do, your honor."

"Go ahead, then."

"Tho Gesed, please take the chair."

Unfortunately, I was the only one who saw the series of reactions flash across Tho's face. In less than two seconds it went from surprise to alarm to fury to control, and then to a sort of forced amusement. If the tribunal had seen it, it might have helped our case. But he didn't, so the only effect was to scare the hell out of me.

Tho's finger floated up to his neck, a gesture which probably seemed like nothing more than scratching an itch to everyone else in the room. His smile broadened as he pulled himself out of his own chair and sauntered over to the witness chair. He didn't take his eyes off mine for a second while the officer swore him in.

"I'm told you have an impressive record at these hearings, Chief. Anyone you arrest is always found guilty."

"Not always, but usually. I don't arrest people without good reason."

"Then you have lost some cases?"

"I have."

"Was Judge Ito the tribunal for any of the cases you lost?"

He weighed me with his eyes.

"I don't remember."

"Let's start with this non-regulation police rod, Chief. You assume it's the work of a sorcerer?"

"Do you have another theory?"

The tribunal intervened.

"That's a yes or no question, Chief. Please answer it."

"Yes," Tho said. "That is what I *assume.*"

"And you also assume a few other things. That there's a sorcerer locally who would create such a device, that Lucky would be able to contact that sorcerer, and that he would have the resources to pay whatever fee the sorcerer would charge. Am I right about all of that?"

Tho chuckled.

"Yes and no, Pastor. All those things happen to be true, but they're more than assumptions."

"Really? How?"

He leaned forward.

"I'm the police chief. You don't think I know what sorcerers are operating locally? I might not have the evidence I need to bring them to justice, but I know who they are. And as for their fee, it could be anything at all. Maybe they'd want some information about things that go on in the parsonage, for example. But in this case it was probably those books. Someone wants them very badly, so there's almost certainly a profit to be had there."

He leaned back and smiled at me.

"So," I said, "you'd have no trouble finding a sorcerer, if you needed one?"

"Not if I needed one. I can't imagine why I would."

"On the other hand, according to Mr. Stevens, Lucky had no idea how to find one. Isn't that correct?"

"According to Mr. Stevens, he was looking. That's the point."

"And you believe that those mysterious books were valuable enough to convince a sorcerer to help whoever wanted the rod?"

"It seems likely."

"When did you first realize those books were that valuable?"

"About the time that people started getting killed because of them."

"Not before?"

"No."

"Do you remember asking me about those books in your office a week ago?"

"I remember asking you about 'contraband,' Pastor. You were the one who first mentioned books."

This wasn't going well.

"Do you remember the deal you offered me that day?"

He looked puzzled.

"Deal? I don't recall any—Oh! I told you that if you'd just turn the contraband over, I wouldn't arrest you. I try not to make things too difficult for upstanding members of the community, especially if it's over something small like possession and a first offense."

"And you promised to give me three days to think it over."

"I can be generous when it's appropriate."

"But you broke your word, and had my house searched the very same day. True?"

He got a calculating look in his eye.

"I can be sneaky when it's appropriate, as well."

"How many detectives were involved in that search?"

"A few. What are you getting at?"

"You must have wanted those books badly, to offer leniency to an 'upstanding citizen' if I would turn them over and keep quiet, then to break your word and expend that much manpower to search my house the very same day. You already knew how valuable those books were, didn't you?"

He was very quiet for a long moment without taking his eyes off mine, and then he sighed.

"Pastor, if you insist on airing your dirty laundry in the middle of this hearing, I can only protect you so far. You had possession of illegal property. I admit to trying to give you a way out of that. But I've been doing this a long time, and I know when someone is lying to me. You were lying, and you were rubbing my nose in it. I admit that it ticked me off. And I'll admit that I went a bit overboard trying to teach you not to flout the law like that. But you'll recall that I never mentioned the word 'books' until you slipped up and mentioned it yourself. The answer to your question is 'no.' I thought I was dealing with a minor misdemeanor and an upstart pastor, who needed to be taught he wasn't above the law."

At that point I just wanted Boyd to show up and bring this thing to an end. But I pressed on.

"You talked to me a second time, after searching the parsonage, true?"

"You mean the time you slipped up and mentioned books? Yes."

"And I explained to you at the time that the reason I mentioned books was that I had found a hidden bookcase in the parsonage, yes?"

"That was your story, after I called you on it."

"And in that conversation you threatened to harm Lucky if I did not cooperate."

"If that's a question, Pastor, the answer is 'no.' I did no such thing."

"You've never possessed a non-regulation police rod?"

"I haven't."

"You weren't trying to get hold of those books yourself?"

"I wasn't."

"Where were you when Will Terren was being murdered?"

"Nowhere near your parsonage."

He addressed the tribunal.

"Your honor, how much more of this do I have to endure?"

The tribunal addressed me.

"Pastor Kinde, do you have any questions left for this witness which you consider to be absolutely critical to Lucky's defense? And, before you answer that, I would caution you that your current line of questioning doesn't seem to be helping his case."

Where was Boyd?

It didn't matter. I had run out of questions anyway. I shot Lucky an apologetic look.

"I don't have any more questions, your honor."

"Very well. Chief Tho, you indicated earlier that you might want to make a summary statement if the pastor made one. Is that still the case?"

"Thank you, your honor. It is."

"Pastor, I am hoping you can sum up Lucky's position—or yours in his defense—in a way that gives the odd series of questions you've just asked some weight in his favor. If that is something you wish to attempt, please do so."

I hesitated. I hadn't done much good for Lucky so far. Part of me wanted a chance to fix that. Another part of me was asking what made me think I was going to suddenly get better at this.

And there was a second danger. I would be giving Tho the last word. What else might he have up his sleeve against Lucky?

I glanced Lucky's way.

He nodded.

I looked at Tho.

He grinned.

And then I saw him again, aiming that rod at Bee's back. I had lost Bee, I had lost my father, I had probably lost my career in the church. I had broken my promise to Anna, whether I ever should have made it or not. I appeared to have lost my chance to help Lucky.

There was nothing left.

Nothing left to lose.

"Your honor," I began, "I don't need to convince you that Lucky didn't commit murder. I only need to convince you that there is not enough evidence to show that he did. My problem, all along, has been that I know who killed Will Terren."

There was a gasp from the room. I continued.

"I know, but I can't prove it. Most of my sources would

never testify for various reasons, and I am the only living witness for some of this story. I've been warned, by those who understand these things better than I do, that it would be very dangerous for me say what I know out loud. So I've been asking questions during this hearing with one hand tied behind my back.

"But Lucky's life is at stake, as well as justice—for Will Terren and for at least two other victims. So I'm going to tell you what I know. It may not be enough to convict the man who committed three murders, but I hope it will at least convince you that the evidence against Lucky is no better than the evidence against someone else."

Dennis caught my eye, and gave me a warning shake of his head. I didn't stop.

"Tho Gesed has been using his office to steal water from the local holder for some time. He's been selling this water to other holders. As part of that scheme he has been providing those users with 'entertainment' in the form of squatter women whom he has coerced by various threats, mostly against their families.

"One of these women—Lucy Ford—discovered that Tho was part of a plot by another holder to rob the Franklyn corporation of its water rights. She tried to use this information to free herself from Tho. It didn't work. He brought her up before Judge Ito, and she was executed for prostitution. She's the first victim in this story.

"Tho's part in the water rights scheme was to get hold of some books, which were apparently being used to bribe someone. I couldn't find out who was being bribed, or why. What I do know is that Tho was promised shares in return for those books. He would become a holder.

"He thought I had the books, probably because he had been watching Will Terren, who also wanted them, and knew about Terren's attempts to find them through Lucky. So he tried to coerce me into quietly turning them over to him. When that didn't work, he threatened to hurt Lucky if I didn't.

"I couldn't turn them over, for the simple reason that I didn't have them. I had never heard of them before his demands. His search of my house turned up nothing. Will Terren came to my house on the day of his death, and searched my office, looking for the books. Tho had been following him. He was killed by a weapon created, by a sorcerer, to look like a normal police rod. Tho has admitted that he knew how to find a sorcerer. And Mr. Stevens has testified that sorcerers create weapons to match the person they are created for—in this case, a policeman.

"I don't know what happened between Tho and Will Terren, but in the end Will Terren was dead. And Tho still didn't have the books. So he followed through on his threat to me, by sneaking the murder weapon into Lucky's room and arresting Lucky. He later told me I could still save Lucky by producing the mysterious books.

"Since I couldn't do that, I set out to find evidence that Lucky didn't kill Will Terren. I was accompanied by a childhood friend—a friend of Lucky's as well—who was visiting the village. With her help we discovered most of what I've told you so far.

"There's just one more piece to this story and then I'll sit down. Late last night my childhood friend visited the Thirsty Angel after hours, hoping to find more evidence on behalf of Lucky. I was worried about her, and followed her there. And I witnessed Tho Gesed killing her with a deadly weapon designed to look like a police rod.

"As you can imagine, your honor, I would very much like for Chief Tho to pay the price for those three deaths—especially for the death of my childhood friend. But I'm not making the case for that. My point is merely that the evidence presented in this hearing, today, supports the story I've just told you at least as well as it supports the case against Lucky. And if that's true, it would be a grave error to convict Lucky based on that evidence."

I sat down.

The die was cast.

Chapter 28

Squatter proverb

JUDGE O'HARA WAS silent for a time, making notes on his Bible. There was murmur of low conversations in the room, and Tho leveled his gaze at me steadily, without any particular expression.

I did my best not to look intimidated.

Finally Judge O'Hara looked up and banged his gavel for silence.

"Well," he said, "I realize that you have no previous experience with hearings, Pastor, so I won't harass you by pointing out all of the ways in which that little tirade was out of line. I would encourage you to get good advice before you venture into any other hearings, and to take it."

Tho was smiling.

The tribunal continued.

"As for the little story you've just treated us to, I can only say that either you take me for a fool, or—"

The back door to the room burst open, and a large man wearing a clerical collar and carrying what appeared to be an over-sized Bible stepped into the room. Boyd was right behind him.

Judge O'Hara watched as they made their way to the railing. For the first time that day he was smiling.

"I'm not through with you, Pastor, but it appears I'll have to deal with this first. So, Boyd Franklyn. What brings you here today?"

Boyd returned the smile. Apparently they knew each other.

"I have a request for this hearing, if I'm not too late."

"Let me hear the request," Judge O'Hara said, "and then I'll tell you whether or not it's too late."

"I request that the accused be given the option of a reading from The Book of Deeds."

O'Hara nodded.

"It's about time someone on his side suggested that. Why wasn't it requested before this?"

"It was, your honor, multiple times. But Judge Ito wasn't inclined to hear what a reading might have uncovered."

"I hope you aren't implying that a tribunal could be anything but impartial."

"No, your honor. Merely that Judge Ito and the chief have worked so closely together for so long that they often find themselves in agreement on legal technicalities."

"Nicely put, holder."

He addressed the large man with the large Bible.

"Hello, Sam. You can take your place."

Sam stepped through the gate and went directly to the reader's desk.

O'Hara motioned for Boyd to sit down.

"You made it just under the wire, holder. I was about to say that the case presented by the pastor in Lucky's defense either took me for a fool, or went directly to the heart of the matter. I would dearly like to find out which."

He turned to Lucky.

"The reader will pray a record of your actions at the time of the murder. I assume that is what you wish?"

"No, your honor."

"No?"

"I don't want any reading."

O'Hara leaned over his desk and looked Lucky in the eyes.

"I need you to understand, Lucky, that if you are, indeed, innocent, then this is the quickest and most direct way to prove it. Without a reading I can't guarantee you won't be found guilty and executed this very day."

"I don't want a reading."

O'Hara leaned back in his chair and surveyed the room.

"It seems I am going to be frustrated at every turn. Very well. Your efforts appear to have been in vain, holder. We'll proceed with Chief Tho's summary."

Tho stood, looked around the room, then at Lucky.

"I have only one thing to add to the evidence itself, your honor. And that is this: An innocent man would never refuse a reading."

I spread my hands toward Lucky in a gesture of apology and helplessness. He jerked his head toward Tho, urging me to act. I didn't know what he wanted me to do.

And then I did.

I raised my stick.

"Your honor," I said, "Might I—"

"Your time for asking questions is over, Pastor."

"It's not a question."

"As is your time for making requests."

"It's not a request."

He was clearly exasperated.

"What is it, then?"

"A suggestion."

He pursed his lips and looked me over.

"Get on with it."

"Your honor was frustrated by Lucky's refusal of a reading. It occurred to me that there's a way around that."

"Yes?"

"The chief has said that no innocent person would refuse a reading. So if he would agree . . ."

O'Hara was smiling again.

"I take your point, Pastor. Thank you."

He turned to Tho.

"Would you consent to a reading confirming your whereabouts at the time of the murder, Chief?"

I watched Tho closely. He would refuse, of course. But at least it would balance the scales for Lucky.

"You want *me* to consent to a reading?" Tho asked.

"We have two people accused of this crime. One officially, one unofficially. It would certainly help me to narrow the field."

A smile spread across Tho's face, and all of the tension went out of his body. He leaned back in his chair, looked directly at me, and moved one finger across his throat.

"If it will help your honor, go ahead."

THE READER BUSIED himself with his large Bible without moving from his desk. One of the officers moved the witness chair back out of the way. After a time, the reader nodded to O'Hara, who prayed the lights dim with a gesture.

A three-dimensional vision took shape in the space between the railing and O'Hara's desk. It was disorienting at first, because the view was angled, as though seen through the eyes of a child looking up at surrounding adults.

The adults were two men. One of them was Matt Anwir, and the other was Tho. Apparently he had his alibi.

But Tho—the Tho in the hearing room with us—objected.

"Your honor, this isn't the time of the murder. This isn't what I agreed to."

It was true, the date and time, hovering over the scene, was yesterday evening. And I recognized the faded wallpaper in Will Terren's room.

Sam, the reader, responded.

"The Book of Deeds answers as it will, Chief."

But by the look on his face, the reader was as surprised as Tho.

Someone was talking in the scene, but it wasn't Anwir or Tho. It was someone we couldn't see. I recognized his voice, though.

". . . highly unlikely, though, of course, we will have to leave no, ahhh, no stone unturned. I do hope, for your sakes as much as my own, you understand, I do hope that your, ahhh, *optimism* is justified."

"They've *got* to be here," Anwir protested. "There's nowhere else they could be."

"As I said, we will do our due diligence. If they are here, we will find them. But if they aren't, as I deeply fear, aren't here, then you know the consequences. Osseus will not be pleased."

Osseus.

Suddenly I was seventeen again, back in seminary, talking to Pastor Dean, the seminary chaplain.

"Osseus," he had said. "A name I want you to forget you ever heard. . . If you ever hear that name again, stay clear of it. Don't get curious, and *don't* try to find out more."

I hadn't heard that name since.

". . . just remember," Brine was saying, "if you do not

produce the books by Monday morning, I will not be able to help you at the meeting, and I assume that your, ahhh, colleague, here . . . I assume he will not be getting his shares."

I wanted to see Brine's face. But he wasn't reflected in the mirror on the wall behind Tho. Then I saw what *was* reflected there.

The door to the room was standing open, and Bee was in the hallway, peeking around the door frame.

I felt a sob coming, but before it hit I saw her eyes grow wide. She pulled back out of sight. But Tho had seen her. He interrupted Brine.

"Excuse me. I'll be right back, sir. I need to take care of something."

And he walked right out of the image.

As soon as he did, the whole image blurred, and a new image took its place.

The date and time was the evening of the murder, during the church service. The view was of the outside of the parsonage, looking slightly downward from above the kitchen door. It was fairly dark, but I could make out the outline of a figure, standing at the door with a hand on the latch. The figure looked toward us, and for a brief moment his face was illuminated by a ragged triangle of reflected light.

Tho.

There was no doubt.

The image faded. O'Hara prayed the lights up.

Tho stared at me, his eyes filled with fear.

O'Hara banged his gavel.

"Considering the evidence presented before us this day—"

Tho's gaze shifted to the judge.

"No!" he screamed, "It's a lie!"

"—including Tho Gesed's reading from the Book of Deeds—"

Tho pointed a finger at me.

"He's a sorcerer! He cast a spell on it!"

"—I rule that Will Terren was murdered by Tho Gesed, and sentence him to death."

It took all the officers in the room to subdue him, including Dennis. The executioner then led the way out to the square.

Chapter 29

Isabelle Jordan, sorcerer

MOST OF THE people in the room followed them out to the square. I hung back. I was in no mood to watch an execution. Even Tho's. I'd had enough of death.

Lucky asked if I would object to a hug. It was good. I hadn't hugged Lucky since I was five.

"You saved my neck, Lad."

"I'm not sure how."

He laughed at that.

"If you don't mind," he said, "all I want right now is to go home to my kitchen."

"Go ahead. I'll be a while. I have people to thank, myself."

Boyd was chatting with O'Hara when I approached. O'Hara saw me first.

"I have to say, Pastor. That was a hearing I'm not likely to forget. But I urge you to stick to sermons from now on."

"I intend to, sir. If I get the chance."

I stuck out a hand to Boyd.

"Lucky asked me to convey his gratitude."

"Tell him it was an honor. I'm grateful to have one victory, at least, this weekend."

"Was that reading any use to you? The part about the books and 'Osseus'?"

"It confirmed my opinion of Brine. But other than that . . . I should be more focused on the board meeting, but between this and Mother . . ."

I nodded.

"Well, I'm going to have a word with Dennis before I go."

O'Hara called after me.

"Remember, Pastor. Stick to the sermons."

I met Dennis at the door to the street. He asked if I wanted to come back for a cup of coffee. I declined.

He squinted at me.

"You're not, are you?"

"Not what?"

"A sorcerer?"

"Are you serious?"

"Of course not. Go home. Get some sleep."

"Thanks for all your help, Dennis."

"I didn't do much—except give you good advice to ignore. I'll see you in the morning."

Had I forgotten another meeting?

"In the morning?" I asked.

He laughed.

"At church. Remember church? Tomorrow's Sunday. Go home!"

I rode my chariot down quiet village streets through the gloaming, usually my favorite time of day. But I hardly noticed.

My mind was full of everything and nothing—the events of the day, my last conversation with Bee, the look on Tho's face when he drew that line across his throat, Boyd's problems, Anna.

It occurred to me that the only one of those I could act on was Anna. I had made her a promise, but I had never even gotten around to praying about her.

I stopped at the church and went in. My steps echoed in the vast dark sanctuary as I made my way to the front and the altar. I sat in the first pew and turned my mind to prayer.

As usual I began by pouring out my concerns and worries. Anna was asking me to commit a sin, and worse, she was asking me to help her commit a sin. But her suffering was real, and not her fault. It did seem she had a point, that if things had been left to their normal course . . . It went on like that for some time, and as God listened patiently to my tangle of worries and misgivings and theological speculations and rationalizations, my prayer became gradually more honest. The issues became clearer. The Gordian knot of my self-deceptions and misconceptions loosened, and began to fall apart.

As often happened in prayer, I began to admit that I was not just there for one reason, but for many. As one thing led to another, I realized I had been wrong, in many ways, about a great many things. Most seriously where I had been most certain that I was right.

I felt like a great cloud of confusion had cleared, that I had been led a good deal further along the path to clarity and love. And God had accomplished it all by a quality of listening.

I rose from prayer tired but refreshed. My mind seemed clearer now, and that may have been the reason that, on the short ride from the church to the parsonage, I allowed myself to think about what I had avoided before. The look of surprise on Tho's face when the reading convicted him. His cry that I was a sorcerer. His absurd claim that the reading itself was a lie.

Of course, if a reading wasn't true, sorcery would be the only reasonable explanation. I had no idea whether a sorcerer could actually manage such a thing, though, or why one would.

And I was reasonably certain that the first scene hadn't been a lie. Everything in it fit perfectly with what I had already discovered. So if Tho was telling the truth—and I had no way of knowing whether he was—he thought something in the second scene was false, the scene that placed him at the parsonage at the time of the murder.

I pictured it in my mind. The dark night, the figure at the door to the kitchen, Tho's face when he looked up.

There was something I had to check.

Instead of going straight into the house, I entered the garden by the side gate and made my way to the shed at the back, where Lucky had his workbench and kept his tools.

I prayed the light on and went directly to a bin where I found what I was looking for, lying right at the top.

It's possible to find the key piece to a puzzle and still not understand how it fits. I had known about my father's stone frog all along, but it had never occurred to me to put it on his magic box, because I had never seen a lily pad when I looked at that box.

The entire picture had been there my whole life, but I had never found the right way to look at it.

Lucky was baking cookies when I came in through the kitchen. He was focused on his work and didn't look up, which suited me at the moment. I went straight through to the stairs and up to my office.

Once there, I closed the door, then I took what I had found in the shed, and I hid it on my desk, under my Bible.

I had the key piece—or *a* key piece—but I needed to find the picture it fit. I leaned on my father's walking stick and went over everything that had happened, piece by piece.

By the time Lucky knocked on my door, I thought I knew.

"Come in."

He opened the door, balancing a plate of chocolate chip cookies on one hand. His way of expressing gratitude.

"I thought you might like a cookie, Lad."

"Thank you, Lucky. Put them on the desk. I want to talk to you about something."

He put the cookies down and his Bible next to them, then stood in front of me, waiting to hear what I had to say.

I leaned forward, both hands on my walking stick.

"You don't like to lie, do you, Lucky?"

"Not particularly."

He smiled at his own understatement.

"So," I said, "you must have been very uncomfortable the last few days."

His smile vanished.

"What makes you think that, Lad?"

"Several things. Do you remember Tho's face in the scene from the reading—the one outside the kitchen door? How we could only see it because something was reflecting light—a sort of triangle of light—from the Joshua on the corner?"

He nodded. I went on.

"A triangle shaped like this?"

I reached over and moved my Bible off the piece of broken window glass underneath it.

He looked genuinely surprised, and for a moment I thought my whole theory might be wrong.

"You're right, Lad. The light must have been reflecting in the broken window."

"Except for one thing. You fixed that window the day before the murder."

"True enough." He had a puzzled look on his face.

"The reading was false, Lucky. That image could not be an image from the night of the murder, no matter what the reading said. I think Tho was executed for the one crime he *didn't* commit."

"It's not evidence he didn't do it, Lad. It's just not evidence that he did."

"True. But there are other things—things I ignored. I started out wanting to prove that anyone did it other than you. Then, the more I learned about Tho, the more I wanted to prove that it was him. And you helped guide me along that path."

"Guide you?"

"You insisted I find out more about Lucy Ford, which led me to learn a lot of very nasty stuff about Tho, but very little that had anything to do with the murder. It did make it easy for me to think Tho was guilty, though."

"I also asked you to find out where that rod came from."

"Yes. And that did have a sort of weak connection to your case, because Tho put it in your room. But it wasn't the murder weapon."

"How do you know that?"

"He used it, or one like it, to kill Bee. And there wasn't a mark on her, let alone a six-inch hole. That was another thing I refused to see, because by then I had an even stronger reason to blame Tho. That may have been why I didn't question the oddest thing that happened in that hearing."

"And what was that?"

"You refused a reading. You had the chance to clear yourself, and you wouldn't take it. Any other time I would have asked myself why. Why would someone risk their life in order to avoid a reading? There's only one possible answer to that."

He didn't respond.

"Did you notice Tho laughing when you told the tribunal you wanted to be called 'Lucky'?"

"I did."

"He thought it was ironic, you sitting in the accused chair. But in the end it wasn't ironic at all, was it? You turned out to be quite lucky."

"I guess so. Now that you mention it."

"And how did you get that name?"

"You know the story. I was working for your father. I had lots of lucky hunches, and eventually it became a sort of joke."

"I don't think they were hunches, Lucky."

I leaned back to take the weight off my walking stick.

"I think you had an information source you didn't tell us about. One you were willing to risk your life to protect."

I pointed the walking stick at his chest.

"I think you had an accomplice."

He looked from me to the end of the stick, and his face went through a transformation. A look of astonishment and understanding, followed by terror.

He knocked the stick out of my hand and dove at me, knocking me backward.

My head exploded with pain, there was a flash of bright light, and then nothing but darkness and a distant scent of woodsmoke.

Chapter 30

"Quietly. We can be heard."

Jeffrey Kinde (Adam Kinde's father)

A FROG SWAM by my eyes. I was underwater, in a lily pond, and I had to figure out how to open the box. It was magic, I knew, and involved untangling a large round knot. Tho was there, aiming a rod at Bee's back. He had large angel wings, and Anna was in her bed. I thought I might somehow use the Lazarus Stone to make Anna and Bee change places. Then Tho would shoot Anna, and Bee would live forever, but I couldn't seem to get the knot loose, and I was running out of breath, and the damn frog kept getting in my way so I couldn't see properly.

Then everything was dark again, and Presbyter Brine was standing over me, slapping my face. I couldn't see him, but I could hear him. All those 'ahhh's. I wanted to tell him to shut up and leave me alone. But first I had to open my eyes. It wasn't easy, but I kept trying.

Finally I got them open.

It wasn't Brine at all. It was Lucky. And they weren't really slaps, more like firm pats. He was trying to wake me.

I managed to mumble, "Whasamatter? Whahappened?" and he stopped.

"Your head hit the wall when I tackled you."

"Tackled me? Why?"

There was a strong scent of woodsmoke in my nostrils. Something left over from the dream?

Lucky was talking.

"I had to. You pointed your stick at my chest. The second I saw it I knew what had happened the first time. I couldn't risk it happening to you."

The top of my head was jammed against the wall. I tried to sit up. Lucky saw and helped me to move so I was leaning against the wainscoting.

The room was still spinning. I tried to focus on his face.

"Either I'm not quite conscious yet, or you aren't making any sense."

"A bit of both, I imagine, Lad. I should probably introduce you. This is Kiarrai."

He moved to one side so I could see. Standing right behind him was a guardian angel.

"Hello, Kiarrai," I said. "It's nice to meet you after all these years."

"'After all these years,' Lad?"

"Help me into my chair."

He did, and in the process I caught a glimpse of a six-inch hole burned into the top of the wainscoting.

I pointed.

"He did that?"

"There wasn't time to stop him. He meant well."

"I hope he's not going to 'mean well' again soon."

The corners of Lucky's eyes crinkled at that.

"He understands now."

"Just to belabor the obvious, he killed Will Terren, yes?"

"How did you know?"

"You were protecting someone, only there didn't seem to be anyone for you to protect. Someone put a hole in Will Terren's chest, only it wasn't Tho's rod, because it didn't do that to Bee. Someone manipulated the Book of Deeds, and that meant something or someone supernatural was involved. Did you know that Dennis heard you two talking in your cell?"

"He did?"

"He thought it meant you were chosen, but I knew you weren't. And then I remembered seeing Kiarrai when I was just a boy, in the woods near your workshop. We—Boyd and Bee and I—assumed Boyd's father must have had a guardian angel. We didn't have enough experience then to realize that important men don't keep a guardian angel secret; they flaunt it."

"And," Lucky said, "that also explained my incredible luck?"

I nodded.

"I may be wrong about this part, but that story about how you saved me from the kidnapper..."

"I was just a street squatter, surviving by my wits. Nothing special about me, and not much hope for a future. Then Kiarrai appeared to me one day, and told me I had a mission from God. It involved a little deception at first, but nothing worse than you'd find in the scriptures. After that I would be helping a good man prosper, and prospering myself. But I was to tell no one about Kiarrai.

"It all happened, just as he prophesied. Whenever your father was facing the kind of difficulty that required information, I would ask Kiarrai, and he would find out what I needed to know. I would have one of my lucky 'hunches,' your father would triumph, and I would rise a bit higher in his esteem.

Until I held a position that would normally go to one of the chosen.

"When your father retired I could have had his position, but Kiarrai said my mission required me to serve *you* now. I was actually glad of that, but then..."

"Will Terren showed up?"

"He was sure you had those books, or were about to get them. Kiarrai couldn't tell me anything about him, which was odd. So I kept meeting him, hoping to find out more. If only I'd mentioned the books to Kiarrai—but I thought he knew everything I did."

I was feeling a bit sharper now. My head had settled down to a dull throbbing ache.

"Stop right there," I said. "That last bit needs explaining."

"Right. I'd always assumed that Kiarrai knew everything—or at least everything I knew. And he usually did, because I had become quite religious, being on a mission from God. I carried my Bible with me everywhere. But it turns out Kiarrai can't go everywhere, or see and hear everything. He can only go where..."

He gave Kiarrai a questioning look.

"I can only be where the Word and Spirit is. I can be many places in my world, but in yours only where it connects to Word and Spirit."

"I'm still lost."

"Mostly," Lucky said, "he visits our world by means of a Bible. I only learned that myself after Will Terren died."

"I can only be in this room now," the angel said, "because there are two Bibles here. If there were none I could not be here."

"I thought he knew Terren was after the books," Lucky continued, "because I assumed he had listened to all our conversations. So it never occurred to me to tell him. But they'd all taken place—"

"—in the Thirsty Angel."

He nodded.

"Kiarrai couldn't go there, because there were no Bibles there. The first time he knew about the books was when Will Terren stole them. I had left my Bible on the coffee table, and when I saw Terren leaving your study with the books I chased him down the stairs. He turned at the bottom, and tried to hold me off by jabbing at me with his walking stick."

"And Kiarrai defended you."

"Kiarrai thought the stick was a dangerous weapon. That's what I realized when you pointed your stick at my chest. Until then I didn't know what triggered him. I was scared to death he'd kill someone else."

"It was not," Kiarrai explained, "made of wood."

"It's monkstone," I said.

"Something like the monkstone a police rod is created from. But not monkstone. I cannot find it."

"Can't find it?"

"I cannot locate it in my world. It only exists in yours. Monkstone would exist in my world as well. I could have stopped it there."

"Interesting. My stick was created by a sorcerer. Will Terren's must have been, as well. So you thought both sticks were weapons?"

"I am Das' guardian."

"I'm still not sure why it mattered that you didn't tell Kiarrai about the books. By the way, where are they?"

Lucky faced the angel.

"He can be trusted, Kiarrai. He might even be able to help."

The angel was silent for a moment, making up its mind.

"The books are my mission. That is my difficulty. I was created Das' guardian in order to locate the books."

We were gathered around Lucky's work table in the kitchen. Lucky and I were drinking hot chocolate. The poor angel could only stand by and watch us. The wooden table was covered in chunks of bread crust, discarded cooking parchment, and a sizable pile of books.

Lucky had been preparing his weekly batch of loaves before Will Terren's death. Kiarrai had begged him to hide the books, not being able to even pick them up himself.

Knowing how thorough a search could be, Lucky hit upon the idea of disguising the books as loaves of bread—wrapping them in parchment and baking a thin crust around them.

I had been so used to seeing a line of loaves on the rack that it never occurred to me to question them. A real police search might have, but Tho's search wasn't real.

"Kiarrai was intended," Lucky said, "to get me hired and trusted by your father, so he could use me to find them."

"Why did he need you for that?"

"Your father was very cautious around Bibles, which made it hard to track what he was doing. I was planted as an unwitting spy, in hopes that I would tell Kiarrai something that he couldn't see for himself. He asked me about my day regularly."

"And Kiarrai's 'difficulty'?"

"We have the books, now. But Kiarrai hasn't reported that to his superiors. It seems that most guardian angels report to the person they're guarding, and their mission is just to protect that person. But Kiarrai is responsible to someone other than me, someone in his world. And his mission isn't just to protect me. So he's caught in a sort of existential conflict of interest."

"My mission," Kiarrai said, "is to find the books. I have to complete my mission. But if I find them, the mission will be over. I will be retired."

"He means he will cease to exist."

"And if I cease to exist, I will not be able to protect Das."

I nodded.

"So you have to choose—"

"Between my mission and my being."

"In other words, you don't want to die."

"Not merely 'being'—'*my* being.' Finding the books is only my *task*. Das' guardian is what I *am*."

"I think I understand," I said, "And I think I can solve your problem. But if I succeed, I'll need a favor from you in return."

Chapter 31

"Kinde's first 'adventure'—if we ignore rumors about his seminary days—occurred in his early twenties, and involved a family servant accused of murder. The records indicate that his triumph in that case was more a matter of luck than skill. But the experience must have added to his confidence, and in that way contributed to later successes."

Silas Redford, *The Real Adam Kinde: An Experiment in Biography*

I TOLD them I was about eighty percent sure I could get things back to the way they were, before the books appeared.

"If I'm right, Kiarrai will be true to his mission, and he can continue guarding you."

"And the other twenty percent?"

"If I'm wrong, Kiarrai will have fulfilled his mission, and

he'll be retired. It's a chance he'll have to take if he wants to escape his current dilemma."

I had compelling reasons of my own to hope they agreed, but I wished I had a way to increase their odds.

In the end, they did agree, and we went to bed. Sleep came easily enough after such a trying day. I didn't dream at all, and when I woke the next morning, I knew at least one way to narrow that twenty percent.

I left a word for Presbyter Brine, and hurried to the church.

I had neglected many of my duties over the last week. Some could be taken care of later, but some I wanted to deal with before the service.

The formal cloth for the altar had been handled carelessly by my substitute the previous Sunday, and I managed to tidy it up and arrange it so that the creases didn't show too much.

Several children were scheduled to receive their Bibles that Sunday, and I had been remiss in clearing out the return bin, so I had to search for those. Luckily there were enough without the initials of a chosen, and I didn't have to do any cleansing rituals.

I had a quick meeting with the members who would be participating in the service.

That was when the panic set in.

Among other things, I needed to show them which scriptures to read, but I didn't have any, because I hadn't written my sermon. There was no time to think, so I gave them the first two passages that came to mind: the beginning of the story of Hannah, and the bit about Joshua's prayer before his stoning.

By then it was time for the service to begin. Between performing my role in the service and my panic over not being prepared, I did very little thinking before it was time to preach.

So there I was, standing in the pulpit, with two scriptures to preach from and not a single word written. I had to speak, so I did.

I made it through that sermon without at any point knowing what I would say next. Both passages dealt with a prayer, so I began by comparing them. That led me to observe that both cases involved less than admirable motives—an observation that could certainly have gotten me in trouble in the case of Joshua—but also honesty, with both self and God. I went on to talk about the importance of that and the value of it to the one who prays.

I went over my usual fifteen minutes, but there was no restlessness in the congregation.

After the service there was a long line of people telling me how helpful the sermon had been—including Simon Fernandez, the clockmaker, who made an appointment with me for 'spiritual counseling,' and Henry from the Thirsty Angel, whom I had never noticed in the congregation before. I had never gotten a response like that one.

And my odds had increased that morning to ninety percent.

The last person in line was Presbyter Brine.

"Excellent sermon, Kinde. Except, of course, the bit about Joshua's motives. Just between us, mind you, there might be something . . . ahhh . . . something not completely heretical there. Given, that is, the proper context. But a service for the laity is not . . . ahhh . . . not the place to air such—such fine distinctions, if you take my meaning."

"I'll keep that in mind, sir. Would you like to walk to the parsonage with me?"

"I take it that you now have—that our walk would not be a waste, that is, of my time?"

"Not if you're willing to promise me two things."

"And these two things would be?"

"If I keep my part of the bargain, I want you to vote with Boyd at the board meeting tomorrow."

"That would not prove an obstacle. If you know about that, you also know that I have already suggested the same arrangement with the . . . ahhh . . .holder—the holder himself."

"Good. And I want you to arrange for the Lazarus Stone to be removed from his mother's bed."

We walked in silence for a time.

"That is a . . . ahhh . . . a different order of request. It might prove difficult."

"Even though it was you who arranged for it in the first place?"

He stopped walking and gave me his appraising look.

"So you have discovered that. Once this matter is concluded, we will have to—you and I should discuss, that is . . . your future career. There are possibilities, definite possibilities in store for you."

He turned to continue walking, but this time I didn't move.

"Can you promise me that?"

"The . . . ahhh . . . the difficulty is that it is much easier to persuade a healer to put a Lazarus Stone in place than it is to persuade him to remove it. But I think, if you can actually produce the, the items in question, then I think I will have the leverage required for that."

"Was that a 'yes'?"

"It was. Can we continue our walk?"

I took him in the front door, and straight up the stairs to my office. The stairs took him a little time, but he didn't complain. The books were neatly piled on top of my desk.

He wandered over to them, picked one up, leafed through it briefly, lifted another to look at the one beneath, then met my gaze.

"These are not the books I need."

One hundred percent.

"I can't help that, sir. These are the only books I know about. I've kept my part of the bargain."

He eyed me again.

"Have you? Perhaps you have. That doesn't, of course, mean that you won't come into possession of the items I'm after in the future. Will you agree to turn them over to me if that were to happen?"

"Absolutely," I lied.

"I can help your holder friend, in that case, at the board meeting. And I can convey to you the news that our . . . our reorganization has been reconsidered. Your position will be secure for the time being. Your other . . . ahhh . . . other request —the matter of Anna Franklyn—presents a difficulty, however. I find myself in a similar position to our last conversation. I would need the items in question in hand, in order to convince the necessary authorities. And since these are not the items . . ."

He picked up one of the books again, examined the cover, and put it down.

"This appears to be the start of a fine collection, Pastor. I would advise you to find a secure hiding place."

I GAVE Lucky the good news over lunch.

". . . so those aren't the books that Kiarrai is supposed to find. And that means he can continue looking for the books he *is* supposed to find *and* continue being your guardian angel. Everything's back the way it was."

"But what if Kiarrai's superior hears about these books? Won't they wonder why he didn't report those?"

"I doubt it. Did he report the books in Boyd's library?"

Kiarrai appeared next to the table.

"No. I was certain they were not the ones I was looking for."

"Eavesdropping, are we?" I said.

"It is part of my mission."

"So," I continued, "there's no reason he should report these. They showed up in that false cupboard in my office—clearly left by a former pastor. But Kiarrai was sent to look for books my father presumably had years ago. The chance that they were the same books was always minimal."

"But he didn't know where they came from."

"He does now, so his conscience should be clear."

"What if they—his superior—asks him?"

"Does your superior ask you questions about your mission, Kiarrai?"

"Not so far."

"There you are, and if he is asked, he doesn't have to say when he knew."

Lucky looked doubtful. "Can an angel lie?"

"This angel can. Remember the scene he tampered with in Tho's reading?"

* * *

"I HOPE you know what you've meant to me."

I was back in Anna's bedroom, holding her hand. She had kicked the healers out, though they were reluctant to go after Bee's attempt to steal the stone. But Anna insisted on a private time with her spiritual counselor.

"I mean it," I continued. "You're going to leave a great hole in my life."

There was a tear in her eye as well.

"You were like another son to me."

She squeezed my hand.

"Now don't tell Boyd I said that; he's the jealous type."

"Did you get to say your goodbyes to Boyd?"

She smiled.

"I can still read, even between the lines. I knew why you were coming, as soon as I saw your word. I told him I had a premonition."

"So you're ready?"

"I am."

"And you're sure?"

"I am."

Her Bible was lying on her nightstand, but I had my own with me as insurance.

I squeezed her hand back as I spoke.

"Kiarrai."

The angel materialized at the foot of her bed.

"Fear not!"

I hadn't heard an angel utter those words since I left seminary.

Kiarrai addressed me.

"I have found it."

He turned to Anna.

"Are you prepared, Anna Franklyn?"

She nodded and smiled.

The angel vanished.

She squeezed my hand once more.

The healers burst into the room.

Chapter 32

"There has been a repeated tendency among Adam Kinde's biographers to make him more than human on the one hand, or to claim he must have had access to hidden resources on the other. We have no evidence of either, or that he set out to accomplish all that he did accomplish. He was intelligent, obsessively curious, and willing to go to great lengths to help others, but he was, in the end, still an ordinary human being."

Silas Redford, *The Real Adam Kinde: An Experiment in Biography*

LUCKY HAD supper waiting after the evening service. Lamb chops, roasted tomatoes and carrots, hot sourdough bread. We opened a bottle of red wine.

We talked a bit about the events of the week, but soon found ourselves sharing memories: of my father, of Anna, of Bee. We laughed, we hid our tears, we traded tales—some new, some old. By the end of the meal we ate in silence, basking in companionship, in our return to normalcy, to dailiness, to peace.

After supper I went up to my bedroom and put my Bible on my nightstand. I closed the bedroom door tightly behind me and stepped quietly down the hall to my office.

I closed that door tightly as well, and latched it.

Isabelle Jordan, our sorcerer friend, had said, "When someone who has been both a friend and a patron dies, we choose one of the projects they commissioned, and create a duplicate to remember them by."

One of the projects.

Kiarrai had said, "I can only be in this room now because there are two Bibles here."

Two Bibles.

Lucky's and mine.

When I had searched the return bin before church that morning I had found what I'd expected to find—a Bible with my father's initials.

And Kiarrai couldn't see my walking stick in his world.

I picked up the Bible sitting on my desk—the one my father had hidden away in his secret box.

I signed the opening prayer.

It came alive, even though he was a holder.

I prayed a reference.

Hezekiah 3:18.

A message appeared on the surface.

"When you are in a closed room," it said, "with no other Bibles, pray that verse again."

It vanished, and the Bible was blank again.

I made the sign a second time.

I prayed Hezekiah 3:18 again.

There was no chair on the other side of my desk, but my father was sitting in one.

He gave me a wry smile.

"Well, this is a bit awkward, son. Some of what I'm about to say isn't all that flattering, and you have no way of defending yourself. I apologize for that, but needs must. I don't know whether I found a way to safely tell you about this Bible, or whether you've discovered it yourself. It doesn't matter.

"I hope you know that I've always respected you. You've always cared for others, you've always been responsible, you've always been fair-minded, even as a child. You've always had your own mind, as well, something your mother and I encouraged.

"Pastor Dean is a good man, whatever I think of his beliefs. It wasn't surprising that you were drawn to him, and that you found his beliefs interesting, even compelling. But we were surprised when it turned out to be more than a phase for you, when you went off to seminary. Even more surprised that you stayed. I feared for you when you came back to visit so rule-bound. It felt to me like your mind had become rigid, and weakened by it.

"But I digress. Your religious beliefs are your own business, and I am sure you will eventually find your way—even if it isn't my way. I'm leading up to an explanation here, so bear with me.

"At the moment I say this I am the last Keeper of the Kinde family journals—a long line of men, beginning during what people call the Dark Age. We are a series of fathers and sons, each of whom has kept a journal during their lifetime. Each of whom has handed that journal down to one of their sons, along with all the accumulated journals which were passed on to them.

"For much of that time there was nothing controversial about this practice. But in the period at the end of the Dark Age and the beginning of the Millennium, books—even private journals—were banned. When you read these journals I think it will become clear to you why that was done. There were a great many things that those in power did not want remembered.

"Our ancestors thought some of those things should be remembered, and they did their part by secretly continuing their journals and the tradition of passing them on, even though this was against the rules. They have had to counter constant attempts to steal or to destroy them.

"And that's where my problem lay. You had become a rule-follower. I was willing to respect that. But I also had an obligation to keep these journals safe. I almost decided to do something that tore at my heart—pass these journals on to someone other than my own son.

"Your mother intervened. She's convinced me to trust you in this. So I am. The journals were a collection of worn books when I received them—aging and difficult to hide in their original form—so I had this Bible made. It's a remarkable work of sorcery—another breaking of your rules, I'm afraid. When we're finished here you will find that your initials have replaced mine on the front. You are now the Keeper, whatever you decide to do.

"It can replace your Bible in all respects. Don't ask me how —I'm a complete amateur in the ways of sorcerers. There are only two differences. The first is that by praying the verse you just prayed, you can see a page that isn't in your current Bible. It contains instructions on how to use this Bible, an index of the journals of your ancestors, and a way to add your own. The second difference is that I am told, by one who should know, that those in power can eavesdrop through normal Bibles, and that this one is safe from that. So it's the safest hiding place I can imagine. Unless someone discovers that you possess two Bibles rather than one it should be undetectable. It has been, for me.

"Now your mother has something to say. Good luck, Son."

He faded away, and my mother took his place. She didn't

look well at all. They must have created this word sometime close to her death.

"Hello, Adam. I don't know if I'll see you again in the flesh, so this may be my chance to say goodbye. You know I love you. And I know you love me. We're both proud of the man you've become. I've convinced your father to trust you. Please trust yourself. If you do, I have no worries. You'll do the right thing, rules or no.

"Do you remember my friend Joan—Beth's mother? You called her 'Aunt Joan' when you were a child. She doesn't know about these journals of your father's, but she can be trusted absolutely. I've asked her to visit you when your father dies. She'll help you decide, if you confide in her, and if you don't, she'll still be a great help in other ways.

"I do hope I'll see you again, but if I don't, have a wonderful life. Goodbye, Darling."

She blew me a kiss, and was gone.

So, tears again, and then I perused the index. It was tempting to begin reading—if not from the beginning, at least from my father's entries.

But I had a lifetime for that.

First, I had mourning to do.

I thought about all those who had died in the last two weeks. Lucy Ford, facing down the executioner. My father, unsure of whether to trust his son. Will Terren, surprised by an angel while robbing a parsonage. Tho, confused and furious and terrified of the very sorcery he had used against others. Anna, relieved and grateful for death.

And Bee.

Bee, granting me that smile in the Humble Monk, trying to steal the Lazarus Stone, arguing theology with a seminary graduate and usually winning, resting her head on my shoulder with the rain pounding against the windows.

Bee, lying on the pavement as the ambulance turned black.

Bee, not just dead, but erased—as though she had never existed.

What had Dennis said? "She was a Human—an infidel. They apparently retrieve their own dead."

I pictured Will Terren, lying on a table in the police station basement.

Why hadn't they retrieved Will Terren?

Something about it didn't make sense.

The End.

I hope you enjoyed *The Human*.
May I ask for a very quick favor in return?
Reviews make a huge difference for authors, helping to sell our books so that we can keep writing more.
If you could take a second to leave a rating and a couple of words giving your honest review, it would mean a great deal to me.
This link should make it easy:
Review The Human

All my best,
-krw

ALSO BY K. R. WATTS

The Guardian Dolphin

Parables from the Grave

Human Unforgiven

ABOUT THE AUTHOR

K. R. Watts is the author of two series, *Philosophical Fantasies*, and the *Adam Kinde Alternate Future Mysteries*. He graduated from California State University at Northridge, and received an MA in theology and a Ph.D. in philosophy from Fuller Theological Seminary in Pasadena. He and his wife Virginia have two children and three grandchildren.

 facebook.com/krwatts1